CLOUDS OF PRAYER

Clouds of Prayer

Copyright Jenny Glazebrook, 2015

Published by Jenny Glazebrook

www.jennyglazebrook.com

Gundagai, NSW

Typesetting by Book Whispers www.bookwhispers.net
Cover design created by Kremena Petrova (k_petrova84, elance).

National Library of Australia Cataloguing-in-Publication entry (pbk)

Author: Glazebrook, Jenny, author.

Title: Clouds of Prayer / Jenny Glazebrook.

ISBN: 9780992536343 (paperback)

Series: Glazebrook, Jenny. Aussie sky. 3

Target Audience: For young adults.

Subjects: Man-woman relationships--Fiction.

                Interpersonal relations--Fiction.

                Young adult fiction.

Dewey Number: A823.4

All characters in this publication are fictitious.

All rights reserved. No part of this publication may be reproduced, stored in, or introduced into a retrieval system, or transmitted, in any form, or by any means (electronic, mechanical, photocopying, recording or otherwise) without the prior written permission of the publisher.

CLOUDS OF PRAYER

Aussie Sky Series

Jenny Glazebrook

To my Dad,

It's almost six months since you went home
and I miss you more than I ever thought possible
but there is comfort in knowing that Jesus came and got you,
never leaving you alone for a moment.

I look forward to the day I will also meet Jesus face to face,
when we will enjoy eternity together with Him, our closest friend.
I love you and miss you and will see you then.

CHAPTER ONE

Rachel knew she was running out of time. She threw her school bag down beside the piano. 'Twenty minutes. That's all I've got.'

She grabbed the sheet music from her bag and tried to straighten the wrinkles. She should buy a folder to keep it in. The noise of other students outside enjoying their lunchtime wafted in and she smiled. Now she should be able to practice to her heart's content.

She had only just touched her fingers to the keys when a strange sound came from the roof. Something like footsteps. Surely someone wouldn't be silly enough to be on the roof of the school music room? It was steep and slippery. Even the unruly Brad Jenson had never dared climb up there to rescue his tennis ball. She must be imagining it.

Rachel strained her ears. Nothing. She closed her eyes and commenced playing, building to a crescendo and then dying down again. Her heart and soul went into the music as she allowed herself to enter another world. However, that world was different today. There was an uncharacteristic beat and it was out of time. Her fingers hesitated on the keys. What on earth was that? The beat hadn't been in her imagination – there was a rhythmic thump, thump, as though something was being bounced down the roof. She looked out the window and saw students rushing from every direction until a crowd had gathered. She raced outside.

Her cousin Kylie was amidst the crowd and Rachel made her

way over to her. Kylie pointed up to the top of the roof. 'One of those new kids from the circus is up there.'

Rachel joined the necks all craning to see the dare devil 'new kid'. He stood barefoot, balancing easily on the ridge of the roof, throwing down balls one by one.

Rachel had heard about the new students but hadn't met them. 'I think his name is Prince, isn't it?'

Kylie nodded. 'Yeah. According to the rumours. Or is it Storm? No, I think that one is Prince.'

'It's Prince.' Another student joined in their conversation. 'Storm is the younger one.'

The accumulation of hand balls and tennis balls finally came to an end and Prince hesitated. Rachel held her breath, wondering how he'd managed to get up there in the first place and how he planned to get back down without breaking his neck. To her surprise, he walked along the ridge, keeping perfect balance. Each step he made was risky but confident.

Then he stopped, looked in her direction and waved. Rachel felt her heart skip a beat. Why would he be looking at her? Then she realised; of course he wasn't looking at her. He would be looking at her cousin Kylie, just like everyone did. Kylie's natural blond ringlets and deep turquoise eyes caused a stir wherever she went. As usual, she was wearing mascara, light eye colour and lip gloss that enhanced her natural beauty and went against every school rule.

'What's he doing now?' Kylie's voice was breathless. Rachel shrugged, unable to tear her gaze away from the teenager on the roof. With practiced ease, he poised his athletic body for a back flip. Then at the last second he seemed to change his mind, producing a string of cartwheels instead. He came to a stop and one foot slid from under him. Rachel held in a scream. There was a chorus of gasps but Prince managed to right himself without effort, casting around a cheeky grin. That grin made Rachel wonder if he had done it on purpose, just to scare them.

'Please God, keep him safe. Don't let him fall.' The prayer escaped her lips. Prince arched his body forward, putting both hands on the steep slope in front of him. Rachel prepared for whatever might come next.

'Prince Clements! Come down now.' The shout from the teacher startled the crowd and for the first time Rachel realised just how tense she really was.

All eyes turned to Miss Sanders, who now stood amongst the crowd of students. 'But come down slowly.'

With a defiant grin, the new student ignored the teacher's command and began dancing down the roof, finishing with a somersault that left everyone gaping in disbelief. With precise movements, he swung from the gutter and slid down a pole to the ground. Rachel stared. Had she really just seen that? How on earth had he managed to hold himself upright on that roof?

'Put your shoes on and go straight to the office.' Miss Sanders still sounded firm, but there was no missing the tremor in her voice. Prince's nod was compliant as he pulled on his riding boots. He looked up and his eyes locked with Rachel's for a moment before he turned to the girl closest to him. 'Which way is the office?'

With an eager smile, the girl offered to take him.

Rachel headed back to the music room, shaken. She tried to push Prince Clements' charming smile and dark, appealing eyes from her mind. She had music practice to attend to. She set up her music, but found herself merely staring at the piano keys. Prince had charisma that drew her to him. She'd never felt such a strong attraction to anyone before. What was even more disturbing was that she knew every girl in the school would be feeling the same. It was clear he was used to attention and thrived on it. He was a born charmer and performer. So what were he and his family doing in this small, country school?

***

3

Rachel sighed. The bell for class had sounded way too soon. She hadn't eaten and she still hadn't perfected the song she was writing. She had been hoping to get it done today but the arrival of Prince Clements had ruined that plan. Her home life was chaotic and about to get much worse. She sighed again as she took a seat by the classroom window and set her pens out on her desk. History. How could she focus on history when her mother was in hospital and she still had a song working through her mind?

'Oh look, it's piano girl and she's sitting here all alone.'

Brad Jenson sauntered into the room. He was giving Rachel his usual look of disdain. She kept her head down, not bothering to respond, and hoping he wouldn't sit next to her. Thankfully, he took a seat in front while the classroom began filling up.

Brad turned in his chair and his eyes widened as he pretended to gasp. 'Actually, no, Rachel, you're not all alone. Look, who's that beside you? Oh, it's God himself.' He grinned. 'Can you see him? I can't, but I'm sure I heard you talking to him earlier. What was it? Something like, please keep that gorgeous circus boy safe because I would just die if anything happened to him!'

He pretended to swoon and Rachel closed her eyes. If only the teacher would hurry up and get here.

'Mind if I sit here?'

Her eyes flew open at the unfamiliar voice and she felt her face burst into flame. Looking down at her was Prince Clements himself. He was indicating the seat beside her and his eyes were warm and amused. There was no way he could have missed Brad's mocking words.

Brad jumped up. 'No, don't take it, Circus Boy. She always saves that seat for God. He's her invisible friend.' He rolled his eyes and gave Prince a meaningful look.

Rachel tried to speak, but no words came out. Prince gave Brad a bemused look. 'I figure God won't mind standing for this lesson and this is the only seat left.' He shrugged. 'I've got no choice.'

Of course. He wouldn't be sitting next to her if there were any other seats available. Rachel couldn't look at him as he sat down and began pulling items from his school bag. The smell of horse wafted up and she wondered what smelled, him or his belongings? It wasn't an unpleasant smell exactly but it was unfamiliar.

'This is History, isn't it?'

Rachel knew she couldn't ignore him now. She would have to manage some kind of response. It should be Kylie there. Kylie would know exactly what to say. In fact, she could rival Prince himself with the charm factor.

'Yes.' Rachel swallowed hard. 'And sorry about what Brad said. I didn't really … well, Brad just makes stuff up.'

'So you're not really the girl who was playing the piano when I was on the roof?'

He had heard?

He smiled and it reached his dark eyes. 'It was good. I saw you come out of the room and thought it must've been you.'

Rachel nodded. 'It was me.' She gave him a self-conscious smile. 'Though I wouldn't have thought you could recognise anyone from way up there.'

'You'd be surprised what I saw from up there. I got a pretty good view of everything. Maybe you should come up there with me sometime.'

His eyes twinkled and Rachel bit her lip. He really did have the charm thing sorted out.

'I was worried,' she admitted. She might as well put it out there. 'Brad must have heard me pray out loud. But I just prayed you would be safe. Nothing else.'

He nodded and one corner of his mouth lifted. 'Of course. Nothing else. Why would I expect you to pray anything else?' Rachel felt herself becoming warm under his gaze. His genuine amusement was so self-assured. If Prince was going to sit with her every history lesson she might never be able to think straight again.

The teacher arrived and Rachel pretended to be concentrating. To her relief, Prince let her be. The school day was almost finished and she was desperate to get to the hospital to see how her mother was. She stared out the window and then looked harder. Horses were in the paddock next door to the school and they weren't just any horses. They were magnificent creatures and they were cantering along the fence line as though watching and waiting for someone. Two white horses stood out amongst the brown. Rachel's favourite Bible story flashed through her mind. When she was really young she and her father would read together the story of Elijah being taken up to heaven in chariots of fire pulled by horses. The horses looked just like the ones she had imagined. The wind picked up and Rachel almost expected to see the horses rise up into the air in a whirlwind like in the story. She started as one of the larger brown horses came up close to the window and appeared to be looking through, right at her.

'That's Regal Zion.'

Rachel looked at Prince in question.

'He's my horse. He always has this sense of where I am. I could be halfway across the other side of the world and I reckon he'd find me.'

Rachel looked back to the horse. He did seem to be looking at Prince.

'He's not used to me being away from him for so long. He doesn't like this school thing anymore than I do.'

Rachel heard the wistfulness in Prince's tone and her heart went out to him. 'Are you going back to the circus? I mean, you won't be staying here in Everdeen, will you?'

Prince shrugged. 'Not if I can help it. I'll be gone as soon as I finish school, anyway. We're supposedly here to get a better education.'

'Here? Most people go to the city to the private schools for that.'

Prince nodded. 'Yeah, but most people don't have horses.'

He had a point. No city school would have a paddock next door to the school for horses to roam while their riders got an education.

'Well, I hope you like it here. I do.' She kicked herself inwardly. What a stupid thing to say. 'I mean, I don't mean I hope you like it because I'm here, I just mean, I was just being polite.' Her eyes widened. 'I mean, I meant what I said, I just –'

His fingers touched her arm for the briefest of moments. 'Hey, it's okay. I get it. You're being friendly but not too friendly. You don't have to explain everything you say. I'm not out to deliberately take you the wrong way.'

'Thanks.'

'And you don't have to worry about me. I'm used to doing backflips on the back of a cantering horse. I didn't really slip on the roof. I was just mucking around.'

She had been right. She shook her head and he grinned.

'So no more praying for me out loud, okay? I don't need it and you don't need that guy up the front there hassling you.'

Rachel smiled. 'Okay, no more praying out loud.' She wouldn't promise no more praying for him because that was something she would probably be doing every day.She tried not to look down at her arm where his fingers had been. She felt the warmth spread through her and go straight to her heart. What was wrong with her? Seriously, he was just another student.

But as the bell went and she jumped up, she knew he wasn't just another student. The truth was, she'd never met anyone like him.

***

Rachel raced into the hospital, wondering if her mother would still be in the same room. Maybe they'd moved her? Maybe she was too late?

'Rachel?' Her father came out to meet her and she threw herself into his arms.

'How's Mum? Has she –'

'No, nothing has happened yet. Still waiting.'

'Can I see her?' The way he hesitated scared her. 'Dad?'

'Yes, you can. She's very tired, Rach.'

Rachel sighed in relief and gave a small smile. 'Don't scare me like that, Dad! I can handle tiredness. I promise not to tire her out with all my talking.'

Her father ruffled her hair. 'All your talking? You're not the talker in this family and you know it.'

She threw him a sideways grin. 'I wonder who could be, then?'

He raised his eyebrows. 'Well, I have to be. A preacher has to speak, you know.'

'But I've heard it said: the less said the more remembered.'

He gave her a gentle shove. 'Go in there, cheeky girl. Your mother's been waiting and asking for you.'

Rachel stepped into the room, then ran to put her arms around her mother, as much as that was possible. Her father was right. She looked tired as she lay there on the hospital bed. And big and awkward. But she was alive and well and so was the baby inside her. The monitor wrapped around her stomach pulsated out the little heartbeat and Rachel smiled. She would treasure this little boy when he arrived. Her mother had lost his twin sister early in the pregnancy but God had graciously allowed this little boy to survive. When sadness at the loss of her sister threatened to overwhelm her she would remember the gift of life – the strong, steady beating of her unborn brother's heart.

'Please God, keep Mum and the baby safe.' Her whispered prayer was urgent. 'And please help me be the big sister this little boy will need.'

CHAPTER TWO

Time to try again. Rachel settled herself at the school piano. Prince Clements wasn't on the roof today – she had checked. All was quiet and she was ready to start.

The door burst open. 'Rach, there's a call for you in the office.'

Rachel turned, wide eyed. Her cousin Kylie stood at the music room door, breathing hard. The girls gazed at one another silently, knowing what this could mean.

'Mum's had the baby,' Rachel finally whispered, only hoping it was so. 'I have a little brother.'

Kylie's eyes expressed both hope and fear as together they rushed to the office. 'I might have another cousin,' Kylie breathed as though hardly daring to speak the words aloud. 'I couldn't stand it if something happened to him.'

Rachel grabbed her hand and squeezed it. 'Me either.'

***

The deputy principal met the girls at the door.'Rachel, you can take the phone in the office.' Rachel grabbed the receiver to hear her father's voice. To her relief, it was triumphant.

'Rachel, you have a little brother. Three and a half kilos, blonde hair and healthy. He looks just like you.'

'And Mum?'

'Doing well. There were no complications.'

Rachel couldn't help the tears that had started to fall. She felt overwhelmed with the news and managed to gulp back a sob. 'Have you named him?'

'Paul Cameron Seton.'

Rachel felt Kylie's arms come around her in a tight hug. All her dreams of a brother had come true. She had never longed for a sister, because she had always had Kylie. She was a cousin and yet as close as a sister could be.

'Thanks, Dad.' She smiled at Kylie through her tears, letting her know it was good news.

'And thanks, God,' her father added.

'Yes. Thanks, God.'

Rachel hung up and grinned around at the staff who had now gathered, waiting to hear the news. 'I have a brother named Paul.'

'Congratulations.' They smiled back while Kylie gave a yell of delight.

'What's going on?'

The group turned at the deep voice. Prince Clements was coming out of the principal's office and Rachel thought he looked tall and regal with his dark hair and strong, steady walk. His name suited him.

Kylie gave him a coy smile. 'Nothing, except Rachel has a brother.'

'Oh? Well, I have two. And three sisters.'

Rachel wasn't sure if Prince was genuinely perplexed by the excitement, but Kylie obviously presumed he was teasing.

'A new brother, you idiot.' She gave him a playful grin. 'As in a baby, not a twin or triplet or quin or quadruplet like you have in your family.'

Prince's mouth turned up in a slow smile and Rachel wished he had smiled at her that way.

'Congratulations,' Prince was saying, and Kylie gave her a nudge.

'Rachel, he's talking to you.'

Rachel managed to look Prince in the eye. 'Thanks.' Were his congratulations a polite formality or was he amused at the fuss over the arrival of another new life in a world already overpopulated? She couldn't tell. It was impossible to read beneath his charming facade.

It was hard to concentrate on school work the rest of that day and Rachel was glad when it was over. She raced through the corridors, pushing through crowds of students. She was nearly out the door when she ran hard into someone.

'I'm sorry!' She gasped, trying to catch her breath. A boy was reaching down to gather his belongings. His books lay scattered across the hallway. He looked up and Rachel's face broke into a smile.

'You're Storm Clements.'

He frowned. 'Yeah.'

Rachel had heard about Prince's little brother, Storm. He was already in trouble for his haphazard, untidy ways. Hearing about him, she wished he were her little brother. But now she had a little brother of her own. 'I've been wanting to meet you.'

'Why?' His expression was blunt. 'Because I'm a circus attraction?'

Put off for a moment, Rachel hesitated. 'Well, not exactly. 'I just heard about you –'

He cut her off before she could finish. 'You the girl who sings?'

'Yes. Why?'

'Just wondered. I've heard about you, too.'

'My name's Rachel.' She offered her hand. His boyish face broke into a wry grin as he shook it. 'You expect me to remember that?'

'No.' She grinned back. 'I'll happily reintroduce myself every time I knock you down in the corridor.'

'Does that mean you're planning to do it again?' He was

trying to glare but Rachel could see there was genuine amusement playing behind his eyes.

'Possibly.' She gave him a cheeky look. 'But right now I've got to go.'

With that, she rushed away, hearing his gruff voice calling after her. 'Watch out, you'll knock someone else over.'

Half an hour later, Rachel stared down at her new little brother. His skin was red and wrinkled and his tiny face screwed up as he cried.

'He's just like you,' her father teased.

Rachel laughed. 'He sure makes a lot of noise for such a little thing.'

'So did you.'

Shaking her head, Rachel turned on her father. 'I'm sure you weren't exactly a quiet little baby either, Dad.'

'He wasn't.' Rachel's mother looked up for a moment as she continued trying to quieten little Paul. 'And he got louder as he got older.'

'Come on, Sarah, you didn't even meet me until we were in Bible college.'

'No, but your parents have told me stories. You weren't exactly an angel.'

'And *you* were?'

'Maybe not then, but you have to admit I am now.'

Rachel smiled at her parents' banter, thinking they couldn't be any happier and neither could she.

***

'Well, you don't need me anymore.' Kylie stretched lazily across Rachel's bed.

Rachel looked up from where she sat on the floor of her bedroom, looking over a music book. 'What do you mean?' Once again she wished she were more like her pretty, extroverted cousin.

'You have your little brother now.'

Rachel laughed at Kylie's melancholy expression. 'I need you for at least another ten years, you crazy cousin.' She bounced across the bed and gave Kylie a poke. 'Paul won't speak for another two years and he won't say anything worth listening to until he's at least ten.'

'What do you mean until he's at least ten? We knew a lot when we were ten, remember?'

Rachel chuckled as she thought back. Perhaps she thought she knew a lot back then, but she knew nothing, really. It wasn't until two years later that life had suddenly made sense. For the first time she had understood what her father preached about every Sunday: that there was more to life than she could ever know but that God knew it all. The God who made and loved her and had died for her. And she could know him as her true, closest friend.

Kylie poked Rachel back. 'What are you thinking?'

Rachel didn't respond. Her cousin was as close as a sister could be but she had been angry when Rachel tried to explain the commitment she had made to God.

'But you are already a Christian,' she had said. 'You've always believed.'

'Yes, but believing isn't enough.'

'What do you mean it isn't enough? Of course it's enough! You don't have to make a fool of yourself by becoming a little preacher. Nobody likes preachers.' She had covered her mouth as she realised her mistake. 'I mean, apart from your Dad, but that's his job.'

Since that day, Rachel had been careful what she said to her cousin, and especially careful that she never came across as 'preachy'.

As Rachel thought back, a melody began to fill her mind. She jumped to her feet.

'That's it! I've got it!'

Kylie sat up slowly. 'Got what?'

'I finally have the song for my exam.'

'For your exam?'

Rachel nodded. 'I have to write a song and perform it for my final music exam. I've been trying to get it together for ages and now it's finally come.'

'Okay, then sing it for me.'

Rachel shook her head. 'I have to perfect it yet.'

Kylie shrugged and Rachel was relieved Kylie let it go. She liked her work completed and perfected before anyone saw it.

Kylie gave Rachel a wistful look. 'I wish I could write like you. Why did you get all the talent in this family? You're so creative!'

Rachel laughed. 'Come on, Kylie, you don't really envy me. You know I'm so quiet and dull in everyday life. I wish I could be as outgoing as you.'

'You're not really dull. You only go quiet in front of other people.'

Rachel nodded. 'Which is a real problem. I'd love to find a special man someday to spend my life with, to share my hopes and dreams, but if I can't even talk to him, I've got no hope.'

'A special man?' Kylie let out a hoot of laughter. 'Listen to you. You've been watching way too many movies.' She came up close, placing a hand on Rachel's shoulder and looking deep into her eyes. 'Believe me, Rachel, one day a man is going to see you for who you really are and that will be it. I'm the one who will be left with no dreams fulfilled, no hope in life.'

Rachel knew Kylie was making fun of her idealistic notions but she was used to it. She smiled distractedly. Her mind was working quickly, creating the song she would write down the first chance she got.

CHAPTER THREE

Rachel was so keen to get her song written she rushed into the school music room early the next morning before school. She had penned down the words late the night before and now the music flowed, giving her confidence and satisfaction.

Rachel glanced back over the words on her notepaper. *It's not my song, she acknowledged. It's too deep to have come from me. I know God has given it to me.*

She sat down at the piano and straightened the stool, then poised her fingers over the keys.

'What are you doing?'

Rachel jumped at the deep, male voice and turned to see Jeff Randall enter the music room. Jeff Randall had the deepest voice she had ever heard but he didn't talk much. Kylie claimed she had heard him sing and said she had never heard anything like it before.

'I'm writing a song for the exam,' Rachel tried not to blush under his gaze. She never seemed to be able to act naturally around the opposite sex.

'But I'm on the roster.' He jabbed his finger at the piece of paper hanging on the door.

Flustered, Rachel went to look at the roster by the door and Jeff followed her.

'Here.' He reached over her to point out the date and his name clearly written beneath it.

Rachel ducked out from beneath his arms and turned to face him. 'Sorry.' She could feel the fire in her face. 'I must have, um, I was just so keen to get this song written, and well …' She swallowed hard, aware she was stammering like a fool.

He gave a sudden grin. 'Hey, it's all good. Just get your things out of here within ten seconds and I promise not to hurt you.'

Rachel managed a smile, unable to help glancing at his biceps and hoping he never had the desire to harm her. Jeff Randall was one of the members of her class she avoided at all costs. His muscular build and good looks had her intimidated from the day he arrived at their school two years ago. She had also heard he sang in nightclubs and was a brilliant dancer – two things Rachel felt she never could or would do.

'Hey!' he called as she headed out the door and she wondered if he even knew her name. 'You forgot this.'

She turned back to see the sheet of paper he was studying. Her incomplete song.

'Thanks.' She grabbed it from his hands before he could read another line and rushed out the door without another word.

The day went along as normal until lunch time when a shout that was becoming familiar came across the schoolyard.

'Come and see what that circus kid is doing!'

Kylie and Rachel both jumped up to follow the crowd. It didn't take long to see what was going on. Prince Clements was in the yard beside the school, standing on the back of a cantering horse. Rachel could see it was Prince's horse, Regal Zion.

'Montford Express!' He called to one of the white horses which obediently made its way over. Soon it was cantering beside the magnificent creature Prince stood on. With a shout, Prince jumped from one horse's back to another.

'He's amazing!' Kylie whispered. Rachel nodded in agreement.

Then came an angry female voice through the crowd. 'Hey, what do you think you're doing?' Everyone turned to look as

Prince's younger sister, Beauty, rushed to the fence. Her face was pinched with fury. 'Get off my horse!'

Prince merely grinned and did a back flip off the horse and onto the ground. Beauty jumped the fence and rushed to the white horse while cursing at her brother. Slowly the crowd moved away, just as a teacher arrived. Rachel was relieved Beauty had stopped her brother before the teacher had arrived and once more landed Prince in trouble. Why she would care so much she didn't know or understand.

Rachel couldn't help glancing at Prince throughout the classes they shared. Two of his sisters – his triplets – shared some too. Misty was an elegant, smiling girl with dimples, and Starre was a beautiful, poised girl who could have been on the front cover of any magazine. Looking at them, Rachel felt plain and wondered why Prince would ever take any notice of her. But he did. He sat beside her in History, declining invitations to sit with any other classmate. Rachel had never met anyone who appealed to her as much as he did. It appeared that many girls felt the same, as one after another, they vied for his attention. It amused Rachel that his triplets noticed and were clearly not impressed. The dimpled one rolled her eyes and Starre, the prettier one, glared at each of the girls in turn.

'We're here to get an education, not find love,' Rachel heard Starre chastise her brother in their Maths class. He had just smiled his charming smile at Kylie and agreed to sit with her.

Prince raised his brows. 'Speak for yourself.' He dragged his desk to sit beside Kylie and Rachel's. Uncomfortable, Rachel dragged her desk back a row to where Prince had originally been sitting.

Kylie looked surprised. 'Hey Rach, you don't have to move.'

'Yes I do. There's no room for anyone to get past.'

'There is! Drag your desk back over here.'

'I don't have germs,' Prince added with a grin but Rachel wasn't willing to risk arousing the teacher's disapproval. She was sure there must be some rule about moving furniture around the room. So she sat behind her cousin and Prince.

'Do you think I'm in love with Prince?' Kylie asked as they headed out the school gate.

Rachel frowned. 'If you have to ask, then probably not. If you're in love, you know it.'

Kylie looked hard at Rachel, her turquoise eyes clearly displeased. 'You sound as though you're experienced in the subject.'

Rachel blushed.

'Are you?' Kylie pressed. 'I thought we shared all our deepest secrets. Or do you have some man I don't know about?'

'No. Of course not.'

'I thought not.' Kylie's expression was triumphant as she flipped back her blonde ringlets and smiled her playful smile. 'I'm going to ask Prince to go out with me.'

Rachel nodded as Kylie raced to catch her bus but felt her heart sinking. Kylie seemed to be able to attract any man she put her mind to.

At the sound of thundering hooves, she looked up to watch the Clements family head home, riding bareback on their magnificent horses. If they wanted to make a spectacle of themselves, they sure knew how to do it. The school felt more like a circus these days.

*****

Rachel walked toward the hospital, smiling. Her mother and little brother were coming home the next day. Once that happened, this afternoon walk to the hospital would be a thing of the past. She walked in the familiar front door and stopped short. A young man was slumped down on the foyer floor and blood was flowing steadily from somewhere on his head. By his side was Jeff Randall from school. His eyes met with hers and she read fear and desperation.

'Rachel, help us. Go and get someone, please!'

Rachel glanced around. The halls were empty. Where were the staff when you needed them? She hesitated as Jeff pulled off his shirt and used it to try to stem the flow of blood. Without a second thought she ran, calling as she went.

'Help, someone out here needs help!'

She ran straight into a doctor and fell back, winded.

'Where?'

She pointed, then followed, feeling sick. The doctor ran to the patient on the floor. Jeff had turned him over and the sight of his face horrified Rachel. He was so badly beaten there was no way she could recognise him.

'Who is he?' she managed to ask Jeff in barely a whisper.

Jeff's face was white. 'My cousin. A bunch of guys just jumped out of their car and bashed him.'

The doctor pressed a button on the wall and people appeared out of nowhere until a crowd surrounded the injured man. A nurse told Jeff to stay where he was and then disappeared along with the rest. Rachel was left standing there, stunned. Jeff looked as shocked as she felt.

'You alright?' she managed to ask.

Jeff nodded, but he was shaking. There was blood on his hands and she watched as he wiped it down his trousers.

'Can I do anything?'

He took a deep breath. 'No, I don't think so.' He changed his mind. 'Stay with me until they get back?'

Rachel nodded and he headed to the closest seat, sinking down into it. She followed, not knowing what to say. She found herself praying silently, begging God to help Jeff's cousin. She had no doubt that if he survived he would be scarred for life. She tried to get the awful image of his battered head and face from her mind, but it wouldn't go away.

A policeman came in the front door and a nurse directed him to Jeff. Rachel heard Jeff falter as he tried to explain what had happened. The policeman waited patiently, then asked if Jeff could give a description of the perpetrators. Jeff seemed on edge.

'Maybe. No, I don't know. I've never seen them before.' He closed his eyes tight and rubbed his forehead in an agitated way.

'I can't understand why they would do that. It just doesn't happen here in Everdeen.'

Rachel agreed. Things like this didn't happen in the quiet little town of Everdeen. Not before now.

'Rachel?'

Rachel turned in relief at the sound of her father's voice and flew into his arms.

'We've been waiting for you. Your mother and I were getting worried.'

Rachel pointed to Jeff. 'His cousin got attacked. I said I'd stay with him for a bit.'

Her father's brows rose as he went straight to Jeff and the policeman. 'I'm a church minister and a chaplain here at the hospital. Can I help in any way?'

Good old Dad. He was always coming to the rescue. A nurse arrived and directed Jeff and Rachel's father into another room. Rachel gave them a wave.

'I'll let Mum know what's happened.'

Dad nodded. 'Thanks.'

Shaken, Rachel headed to her mother's room. It was good to see her lying there with little Paul. She took her baby brother into her arms, felt him snuggle in contentedly, and stroked his soft blonde hair, Rachel felt that all was right with the world again.

⋇

Rachel hadn't slept well as images of Jeff's cousin assailed her tired mind. The class was waiting for their teacher and she wished she could just go home and sleep. There was no way she could sleep in this classroom. Brad Jenson was throwing pieces of screwed up paper at a student by the name of Bonnie Blake. He and Bonnie had been rivals from their first day of kindergarten, but today Bonnie was ignoring the disappointed Brad. Finally bored by the lack of reaction from the popular girl, he turned to face the rest of the class.

'Did you hear about that gay bashing yesterday afternoon?'
Many heads nodded.

'He was Jeff Randall's boyfriend.' Brad seemed to take great delight in giving the information.

'Who says?' That was Bonnie Blake in her usual challenge against Brad. 'I heard it was his cousin.'

Brad grinned. Finally he had got her attention. 'My Dad told me. He knows the guy.'

Bonnie snorted. 'As if your Dad would know anything. He's just the principal, not Prime Minister.'

All fell silent until Sarah May spoke up. 'It's so hard to believe anyone could treat another human being that way. I mean, even if we have different values, they're still human.'

'Are they?' Brad earned himself a slap from Bonnie and Rachel chuckled, wishing she had the courage to be so forward.

'Don't you laugh, God-girl.' Brad glared at Rachel, rubbing his arm where a red streak had appeared. 'You don't like gays any more than I do.'

'I don't know any,' Rachel responded timidly, cowering under everyone's gaze, 'but if I did, I'd probably like them.'

'As if!' Brad sneered. 'You're totally against it. Your faith says it's unholy and sinful, remember?'

'I don't agree with homosexuality,' Rachel agreed, 'but even God loves those who practice it.'

At her words, Brad let out a shout of laughter. 'You're so proper, aren't you?' He sniggered. 'Like a well-trained record. But you can't help it. Your daddy's a preacher and you've got his genes.'

Rachel blushed deeper and wished she could hide. To her relief, Bonnie Blake stepped in and once more silenced Brad with her cutting words and superior attitude. Rachel wished more than ever that she were like Bonnie at that moment; that she could think of the right things to say at the right time and not cower whenever someone looked in her direction.

What was it that gave Bonnie confidence? Why couldn't she have it too? After all, she had two parents who loved and supported her, and a God who loved her more than she could ever understand. Her life wasn't messed up like Jeff's cousin's. The only grief she had ever been through was the loss of her unborn sister five months ago.

'Lord, help me be confident,' she prayed. 'Help me care so much for other people that I don't even think about what they think of me.'

CHAPTER FOUR

As Rachel sat in the class study, she looked to where Bonnie Blake was chatting with Prince's triplets, Starre and Misty. The popular, blue-eyed Bonnie seemed to be the only one who could make friends with the two reserved circus girls. Rachel longed for a friend who could share her own hopes and dreams, someone who understood her and her faith in God. As she thought, she began to pen down a poem. The faster the words came, the faster she wrote. With a smile, she sat back and read what she had just written. Then to her horror, the piece of paper was snatched from beneath her nose.

'Just one friend?' Brad laughed. 'Don't you think you're asking a bit much?'

Rachel looked down, wishing Brad would leave her alone. Ever since he found out she was a Christian, he bothered her. It was true that he teased everyone, but it was different with her. She could tell his harassment stemmed from a genuine dislike. And now, as she tried to retrieve her poem, he moved further away and began to read it out in a pleading, mocking voice.

'Just one friend for these evenings alone
When emptiness clouds every star
Someone who shares every feeling I own
Receiving them just as they are.

Just one friend to share all my dreams
To know me deep down inside
Someone who knows what hurt and pain means
To share all the tears that I've cried.

Just one friend who will let me be me
Who will love the person I am
Someone who though I'm often confusing
Tries always to understand.

Just one friend to share every sunset
And the stillness of each dawn
Someone to comfort when I am upset
To remind me I am reborn.'

Rachel cringed, waiting for the taunts and laughter. None came. Instead, Bonnie Blake moved to look at the paper, then turned to Rachel with admiration in her bright blue eyes. 'Hey, that's good.'

Many heads nodded in agreement, but all Rachel could see was Brad's mocking face as he taunted her with the piece of paper.

Brad waved the paper in front of her face and took something from his pocket. It was a lighter.

'Give it back to her,' Bonnie commanded fiercely.

Brad ignored her. He looked directly into Rachel's eyes and flicked the lighter until the flame flickered steadily, then moved it toward the paper.

'I said to give it back, idiot!' Bonnie grabbed the poem and the lighter from him and shoved him against the wall. Clapping and cheering broke out then stopped abruptly as the teacher stepped into the room. For a moment, amusement crossed Miss Sanders' face as she took in the way Bonnie had Brad pinned against the wall. Then she hardened her expression.

'Get outside, both of you. I'm tired of you two heckling each other.'

'He was –' Bonnie began to defend herself, but Miss Sanders cut her off.

'I've had enough of your disruptions today, Bonnie. First in Geography, now this.'

Bonnie shrugged and headed outside, followed by Brad. As soon as Miss Sanders left, Rachel ducked outside to where Bonnie stood on detention.

'I'm sorry I got you in trouble.'

'Hey, it's not your fault.' Bonnie shrugged. 'Miss Sanders is more annoyed about Geography, anyway. I spent the whole lesson outside again.' She grinned and Rachel wondered how someone who spent half her school life standing outside the class room could be top of the class.

As Rachel stood outside the school gate waiting for her bus that afternoon, she watched Prince Clements and his sisters head her way with Bonnie Blake in their midst.

'I'll never be like her,' Rachel acknowledged, watching as the popular girl laughed at something one of the triplets said. 'And Prince Clements won't even remember me when school finishes.'

As though hearing her thoughts, Prince slowed as he came by her. His dark eyes met and searched hers for a moment before he said, 'I liked your poem, Rachel.'

Rachel took in a deep breath, unable to respond. He didn't give her time to, anyway. He had already continued on his way and was saying something to one of his sisters.

Rachel smiled. Brad could tease her all he liked. She watched as the triplets and twins headed to the paddock next door to collect their horses. They truly were an amazing family.

***

Bonnie Blake and some of her friends were standing by the

canteen when Rachel came in the school gate the next morning. Their conversation caught her attention and she slowed down.

'I've heard he's really religious,' Sarah May was saying to Bonnie.

Who was religious? Were they talking about someone who was a Christian?

She heard Bonnie's voice. 'I've spent a bit of time with him and he's always talking about God, but he's nice, too.'

'But how can a circus boy be religious?'

Bonnie shrugged. 'I don't know, but he sure takes it seriously. He reckons he talks with God and they're friends or something crazy like that. He claims it's not religion because religion is a set of rules but his belief in God sets him free.'

Rachel gathered up her courage. God may have just provided her with a friend who believed as she did. She approached the group, hope filling her. 'Which one believes in God?' The Clements family were the talk of the school, and more than anything, Rachel wanted to make friends with any one of them who happened to share her belief in God.

Sarah May gave Rachel a strange look but Bonnie smiled at her. 'The oldest. Actually, I think he believes pretty much the same as you do.'

Rachel couldn't help smiling. It was as she had never dared hope or dream. The handsome, regal Prince Clements was a Christian just like she was. Perhaps God had answered her prayer for 'just one friend' to share her faith and hopes and dreams. She decided then and there that she could not let this opportunity pass by. She would simply have to ignore her self-conscious fears and invite him to the church youth barbeque her father had arranged for that evening.

Rachel's chance came in history. She took a deep breath as he sat beside her.

'How's it going?' he asked in his friendly, familiar way.

'Good.' She managed to pull herself together. She'd have to

do better than that. 'Where's Regal Zion today?'

Stupid question but he didn't seem to mind.

'Next door somewhere. He's a bit more relaxed now he knows I do come out of this building again to get him at the end of the day.'

'Oh.'

His dark eyes studied her as he gave the friendly, amused look she was becoming familiar with. He was waiting. Waiting for her to say something. This was it.

'Um, there's a church youth barbeque on tonight.' She wished her voice didn't sound so timid. 'I just wondered if you'd like to come and meet a few people.'

Prince looked surprised. 'A church barbeque?'

'Yeah. There will be a few people our age there and I thought it would be nice for you to meet a few other Christians.'

His amused look was back. 'You did?'

Flustered, Rachel nodded, not understanding his look.

He shrugged. 'Well, my brother's going, so I might as well come along too.'

'Your brother knows God?' Rachel pictured the scruffy looking Storm Clements. She had never imagined he might be a believer that day she had knocked him down in the hallway.

Prince nodded. 'Yeah. I should introduce you to him. You'd get along well.'

'It's okay. We've already met.'

'You have?'

'Yeah, a few days ago. I accidentally ran into him.'

Prince nodded and Rachel felt she had talked too much already. Besides, being so close to Prince set her heart beating so fast she couldn't think straight. She needed to stop before she said or did something silly.

'I look forward to seeing you this evening,' she said hurriedly, then bent down and focused on her work.

***

Rachel couldn't settle as she looked around the crowd at the church barbeque. Prince had assured her he would come but there was no sign of him. Then she saw him. At the same time, every other teenage girl in the group did, too.

'It's Prince Clements.'

'What is he doing here?'

'I wouldn't have thought he'd be caught dead here.'

Rachel felt annoyance flood through her. Why not? Couldn't a good looking guy enjoy the company of fellow believers? She faced the girls.

'I asked him.'

They stared in amazement and Rachel managed to look back at them with confidence and even defiance. What was wrong with quiet, shy, Rachel Seton asking Prince Clements to the church barbeque?

'I wouldn't have thought he'd be interested,' a year twelve girl admitted as she stared. 'I knew his brother would be, but not him!'

All fell silent as Prince headed their way, smiling at Rachel.

'I made it.' He flashed his white teeth around at the other girls. 'This is my brother, Blaze.' He pushed forward the tall young man beside him then smiled his charming smile at Rachel. 'I believe you've already met him, Rachel.'

'Well, I haven't,' Rachel confessed, studying Prince's older brother. She hadn't realised there was another member of the Clements family. He wasn't like the others. His face was covered in pimples and his appearance was plain in comparison with Prince's, despite having the same dark eyes and sun-browned complexion.

Prince looked puzzled. 'I thought you said you had met him.'

'I meant Storm.' Rachel was beginning to feel uncomfortable. Something was definitely not right. Her suspicions were confirmed when Prince laughed, then swore.

'You thought Storm was a Christian? He seemed to think the mere concept was uproariously funny. He turned to Blaze. 'I told her my brother was a Christian and she presumed it was Storm.'

Blaze smiled, but Rachel didn't notice. It was all dawning on her. She had made a terrible, embarrassing mistake. The pimple-faced Blaze Clements was the eldest, the religious one. Prince wasn't interested in God. Or was he? After all, he had agreed to come to the church barbeque.

'Well, I've only ever seen the five of you.' She was having trouble breathing normally as she tried to defend herself. 'And there's only five horses.'

Blaze nodded. 'I don't have a horse. Don't worry about it. Lots of people presume I'm not a part of the family.' He grinned. 'I'm too normal.'

'Normal?' Prince laughed again. 'You with your fanatical belief in God? You're far from normal, big brother.'

She felt the red rising up into her cheeks and looked around desperately. She needed space – time to recover and put everything into place. To her relief, her father came over. She stood awkwardly as her father began a conversation with the two newcomers. She heard nothing to begin with, but finally managed to focus. Her father was chatting with them in his usual, friendly way as he rocked the newborn Paul in his arms.

'We're just in town until we finish school, then we'll leave.' Blaze's dark eyes were sincere as he spoke. 'I like this town, but I can't achieve my plans for the future here.'

Her father shifted Paul to his other shoulder. 'What are your plans for the future?'

Blaze answered without hesitation. 'I want to be a minister.'

Prince chuckled. 'And I want to be anything but a minister. This religious stuff is all right for all of you but I definitely don't understand it. I think I'd like to be in television.'

'Producing or acting?'

'Definitely acting. Doing stunts and things.'

Rachel smiled. She could imagine Prince in such a scene. But his older brother as a minister? She wasn't so sure.

From that evening, Rachel avoided Prince Clements. She was embarrassed by her mistake and her disappointment that he didn't believe in God went deep. He wasn't that 'one friend' she had asked God for. Yet why Prince had agreed to come to the church barbeque in the first place was something she simply couldn't understand. Perhaps he wanted to charm the girls there. Or perhaps he just enjoyed a free feed.

***

It was only the next day that Kylie danced up to Rachel with a beaming smile. 'I finally did it, Rachel. I asked Prince.'

'Asked him what?'

Kylie snorted. 'Asked him what? You really are so dense sometimes, Rach. I asked him out. We're going out. We're a couple.'

'Oh.' Rachel tried to keep her face expressionless. So that was it, then. There was no way she could or would try to compete with her pretty, outgoing cousin for Prince's affection. Her own straight blonde hair and serious nature were no match for Kylie's beautiful eyes, blonde ringlets and playful smile. Besides, if Prince didn't have faith in God there was no way he could ever truly understand her or share her life's goals and dreams. Because her life's goals and dreams were all centred around living for the God who gave his life for hers.

CHAPTER FIVE

'Are you avoiding us or something?'

Rachel looked up from the school piano and smiled at Kylie who had Prince's fingers entwined between hers. As if she could avoid Kylie and Prince. They were always there, beside or behind her in class, even in her own home. She felt crowded and the music room was her only escape.

'I'm just finishing this song.'

Kylie rolled her eyes. 'You've been here every lunchtime. You're starved of human company. I mean, does anyone else ever come in here?'

'Jeff comes in sometimes.'

Kylie laughed. 'I meant any normal person who actually talks.'

'I enjoy this, Kylie.'

Kylie opened her mouth to argue, but Prince pulled on her hand, giving Rachel an understanding look. 'Come on Kylie, let the woman write her musical masterpiece.'

Kylie shrugged. 'Fine. I'll come over this afternoon, Rach. You're not babysitting that baby brother of yours again, are you?'

Rachel admitted she wasn't, though she wished she was. With baby Paul in the house, she was busier than ever. Her mother's time seemed to be totally taken up with the noisy little infant, and there was always housework that needed doing. It seemed that Paul had given her the perfect excuse not to spend afternoons in the company of Kylie and her regal boyfriend.

'You here again, Rachel?'

This time it was Jeff entering the music room and Rachel sighed. She couldn't concentrate, now. 'I'm just going.'

'No, wait.' He reached out to her. She stopped as he touched her arm and waited.

'I just wanted to say thanks. Thanks for the other day at the hospital.'

Her brow rose. 'Thanks?' She didn't think she had done anything apart from feel helpless and lost for words as she sat with him. 'Um, no worries. How is your cousin?'

He almost smiled. 'Better than expected. I think he'll be okay. I just hope they find those …' He stopped just short of the unpleasant names he was about to use and shrugged. 'I just hope they do.'

'Me too.' She stood awkwardly, wishing she was like her father and knew what else to say. Instead, she grabbed her music and threw Jeff a wave.

'I'll see you later.'

He chuckled. 'No doubt.'

Rachel wandered outside. She clearly couldn't use the piano and she didn't plan to go and join Kylie and her ever-present boyfriend. She needed a plan C. There was a debate in the library this lunch hour. She would go and watch it.

She wove her way through seats in the library, making her way to the back. She was here to hide. It didn't work.

'How's it going?' Prince's older brother, Blaze, made his way to her side and sat down.

'Good. I'm here to watch the debate.' She glanced at him, wondering at how unattractive pimples could make a person. Blaze would be almost as handsome as his brother Prince were it not for the unsightly red bumps covering his face. Self-consciously she reached a hand to the pimple forming on her own chin, then quickly stopped, realising Blaze might see her action and be offended.

'I came to see the debate, too. I promised Bonnie I would.'

He smiled, and his eyes twinkled. 'Wouldn't dare break a promise to someone like Bonnie, that's for sure!'

'I didn't promise Bonnie or anything, I just came,' Rachel said unnecessarily, but unable to think of anything sensible to say. 'Jeff Randall is using the music room so I had nothing else to do.'

Blaze nodded. 'You spend a lot of time in that music room.'

'I love music.' She was aware she sounded defensive.

'And your cousin loves the male species.'

He was smiling and there was a knowing look in his eyes. Surely he hadn't worked out her true reason for spending so much time in the music room? Was it so obvious she was trying to escape Kylie and Prince's displays of affection? Could Blaze be so discerning?

They fell silent as the debating team entered the room and the debate was underway. Rachel listened, intrigued, marveling at the skill of the speakers. They seemed to be able to think of words and arguments so quickly. She could never think while looking at a crowd of people. Give her pen and paper or a song any day.

Bonnie Blake was the last to speak and her lively humour and arguments kept the listeners attentive and entertained. Blaze was watching her with sparkling eyes and Rachel felt something stir in her heart. She could only dream of someone looking at her that way.

The debate finished with Bonnie's convincing arguments and Rachel turned to Blaze. 'She's brilliant at debating, isn't she? But then, Bonnie's good at everything she does.'

Blaze grinned. 'Not everything. You should have seen her attempt to paint a horse the other day.'

Rachel laughed, relieved to hear there *was* something Bonnie Blake couldn't do.

Blaze suddenly turned to her, his eyes intense. 'Do you envy her?'

Rachel shrugged, then smiled ruefully. 'Well, yes. I guess I do in some ways.'

He put both hands on her shoulders. 'Don't. You and I are

children of God. We personally know God. What more could anyone want?'

Rachel couldn't look away. He was right. He lowered his hands, his look serious.

'Remember Bonnie doesn't have that. But I'm praying for her.'

Rachel felt tears sting her eyes. 'Me too.' She had been praying for most of her classmates for years, and now it seemed someone had joined her in the prayers.

***

It didn't take the Clements family long to adjust to school life and fit in as much as their unusual circus background would allow. They hadn't been at school two weeks before they turned up one day with new haircuts and clothes. Only Storm insisted on retaining his wild mop of curly hair and dirty riding boots.

Rachel couldn't keep her eyes off Prince when he first walked into class with his dark hair neatly cut and his uniform clean and ironed. If she had thought he looked like Prince charming before, he looked even more so, now. And she wasn't the only one to think so.

'He's a good looker,' Sarah May said, then watched, amused, as Kylie put her arms around her boyfriend and kissed him possessively. Rachel didn't know where to look.

'Bonnie took them all shopping,' Sarah May explained, and Rachel understood why the Clements family were now so stylish. If anyone knew how to look good, Bonnie Blake did.

She approached her mother the moment she walked in the door after school. 'Mum, can I get some new clothes?'

Mrs Seton looked up distractedly from where she was feeding baby Paul. 'What kind of new clothes?'

Rachel shrugged. 'I don't know. Fashionable ones.'

'You mean ones that show off your midriff and display your figure for the world to see?'

Rachel frowned, seeing already that it was a hopeless case.

'No, just nice ones that make me fit in a bit.'

Mrs Seton looked sad for a moment and Rachel felt guilty. She attempted to explain.

'I just feel so out of place. I'm different from everyone else at school.'

'Rachel, you're never going to fit in. And you're not meant to. You're a child of God. You shouldn't want to conform to this world.'

'But can't I be in the world and not of it without being ten years behind in fashion?'

Mrs Seton met her daughter's serious gaze and smiled slowly. 'Your beauty is an inner beauty, Rachel. Your gentle and quiet spirit, your love of God. Inner beauty will never fade away. Clothes won't change who you are.'

Rachel nodded. 'No, they won't change who I am, but they will change who people think I am and give me a better chance to relate to my school friends.'

Mother and daughter considered each other for a few moments, then Mrs Seton nodded.

'You can have some new clothes if you want them. I just don't want you thinking they are what makes you of value.'

Rachel smiled wide. 'Thanks, Mum.'

Rachel's father approached her that evening as she sat at the piano. He sat beside her and joined in with the piece of music she was playing. When she finished, she turned and smiled at him, feeling that in sharing her love of music, he understood her heart. She always felt she was travelling to a deeper level of existence in her music. There was a harmony and joy in the sound that could not be expressed in any other way.

'Your mother tells me you're getting some new clothes.' Her father's turquoise eyes rested gently on her – eyes so much like Kylie's. She nodded as she folded up the music.

'Mum's worried I might think my value depends on them but that's not why I want them. I just don't want my friends to think Christians have to be out of date. Living for God isn't about being fashionable or unfashionable.' She grinned. 'And don't worry, I'm certainly not going to buy anything unbecoming of a preacher's daughter.'

Her father smiled then nodded. 'You're becoming quite a woman of God, Rachel.' Admiration and love shone from his eyes. 'I love watching you grow up. You've made me so proud to be your father and yet I know it's nothing I've done. It's God.'

Rachel laughed as she reached over and put her arms around her father. 'God has used you, though, Dad,' she said. 'I have never envied anyone else for their father but I've often wished other people could have a father like you. And now I get to share you with Paul. I love that.'

Her father smiled. 'I think Paul gets a pretty good sister, too.'

CHAPTER SIX

Rachel sat on her hands, wishing they would stop shaking. She hadn't realised just how exposed she would feel sitting at a piano in front of the school hall. The students' chatter faded and her music teacher stood to address the assembly.

'Rachel Seton has written a beautiful song for her exam next week. I have asked her to perform it here for you today.' The teacher glanced at Rachel, then spoke back into the microphone. 'We are privileged to have such a gifted musician in our school and I'm sure that you will all wish her the best of luck with this beautiful piece of music. It is called, "Clouds of Prayer". Thank you, Rachel.'

Rachel managed a smile, and as she began to play, her nerves vanished and she put her heart and soul into her song:

'I see you walking alone in the rain,
feeling tears falling down from above,
and though my God is weeping his pain
you don't know that it flows from His love.

The rain is simply water to you,
a fountain from somewhere on earth,
drenching you wet, soaking you through,
while expressing your heavenly worth.

If only I could share with you
in words you could understand,
but it seems the more I try to get through
the less you can see God's hand.

So I lift you up in clouds of prayer
that are weeping tears like rain,
begging God to help me share
the joy which heals all pain.
I long for you to know His love,
but can't find the words to say
and so my heart is looking above
knowing all I can do is pray.
All I can do is pray
these clouds of prayer.

As she finished, the students and staff burst into applause and Rachel smiled at them. Feeling self-conscious, she closed the piano lid, collected her music and found her way back to her seat. The walk back seemed long, with all eyes on her. She felt herself blushing as Prince Clements smiled and moved his long legs to let her past. If only her song had some kind of positive impact on him. Then she turned to look at Kylie.

'Great song. You're so gifted!' Kylie bubbled, and disappointment knifed through Rachel. Kylie's response seemed so shallow and light-hearted. Feeling tears welling in her eyes, Rachel swiped at them before anyone noticed. Tiredness was beginning to get to her. It wasn't easy to sleep and prepare for exams with a newborn baby in the house. As soon as assembly ended, she made her way to the safety of the music room.

'I just so badly wanted it to have an impact, Lord.' She leaned over the piano. 'But it didn't seem to get through to anyone. Were the words too complicated? Kylie says I'm too deep sometimes. Or did I –'

She startled as Jeff Randall's deep voice came from the doorway. 'I thought your song must have been far worse than that.'

Rachel looked up at him, confused.

'The way you snatched it from me that day, you know, when you were here on *my* day.'

Rachel smiled, knowing he was teasing. 'I was, well, I –'

'It's a great song,' he interrupted, saving her from trying to complete the sentence. 'You sing well.'

'Thank you.' It was the polite thing to say but she felt no joy.

'What's wrong? Don't you believe me?'

Rachel gave a rueful smile, not meeting his eyes. 'I have to admit I was hoping people would notice the words, not just enjoy the music.'

'I noticed them.'

Her eyes widened.

'It's true. I totally get you. I write my own songs and I could tell your heart was in those words.'

'It was.' Rachel sat up straighter, confidence and hope filling her. 'It expressed who I am, really. All that I live for and long for. I so much wish everyone could know God the way I do.'

She hesitated, wondering if she had said too much, but Jeff was listening intently. He started to say something, then hesitated before beginning again.

'It made *me* want to respond.' Suddenly he fidgeted and couldn't seem to meet her eyes. It was the first time Rachel had seen him look less than confident. 'It made me want to know God the way you do. Like, as a friend I can express my heart to.'

His nervous admission took Rachel by surprise. She felt her heart begin to beat faster. This was the moment she had dreamed of and now, suddenly, she didn't know what to say.

'Your Dad spoke to me that day at the hospital. What he said made a lot of sense. He asked if I believed and if I wanted to give my life to God. I think I do.'

'You want to be a Christian?' She had to make sure she was understanding him.

He nodded. 'Should I talk to your father? He's owns a church, doesn't he?'

Rachel suppressed a smile. 'Not exactly. He leads a church and yes, it would probably be best if you talked with him. I'm not really good at expressing myself.'

'You do okay,' he assured her. 'When your heart's in it.'

'But my everyday conversations could do with some help.'

Jeff fought the smile that formed on his lips. 'Yes, they could.' He shrugged. 'I'll talk with your father.'

'Thanks.' She didn't really know what she was thanking him for, except that he had let her off the hook.

***

Rachel arranged a meeting between her father and Jeff the following afternoon.

'Is it okay if I catch the bus home with you?' Jeff asked, and Rachel nodded, wishing her shyness would disappear. She felt awkward with Jeff by her side and yet in another way it felt so right.

He put his bag down on the floor of the bus and settled himself into the seat. 'I've been thinking a lot about this Christianity thing, and I really do want to be in it. I think it's right for me.'

Rachel shuffled in the seat, moving slightly so that his arm wasn't touching hers. 'I hope so.'

That sounded hesitant and the last thing she wanted to do was say something that might change his mind. She sat up straighter. 'Well, I mean, I believe it's right for everybody but I'm hoping you can believe that, too.'

She bit her lip. Did that sound preachy? He turned to face her in the seat.

'Your father offered to pick me up from school but I told him I could just as easily catch the bus with you.'

Rachel nodded. Her father had told her Jeff seemed keen to catch the bus with her. He had then looked at her seriously. 'Is he sweet on you?'

Rachel had laughed outright. 'Dad, he doesn't even know me. We've only talked once or twice in our lives.'

Her father had still looked troubled. Rachel wasn't worried. Her Dad was just being a typical over-protective father. Every father thought their daughter was beautiful and talented and that every boy would desire her. If only.

Rachel sat in her room while Jeff and her father talked, and she prayed hard. 'Please help Jeff get to know you, Lord. Help him understand Dad's words.'

As she prayed, the thought crossed her mind that perhaps Jeff Randall of all people was the answer to her prayer. The one friend to share her sunsets, her beliefs. She let out a chuckle as she thought of her father's concern that Jeff might be attracted to her. How could he be? Long, blond hair and a sweet smile meant little if you didn't have attractive eyes and a slim, elegant figure. From the day Kylie had said her plain, light brown eyes made her look like a lion, she had been very conscious of them. If she looked more like Kylie, or even Bonnie Blake with her wide blue eyes, she might be noticed.

Rachel heard the front door and knew her father was taking Jeff home. What had happened? Did Jeff understand? It seemed an eternity before the sound of the car motor returned to the drive. Rachel ran out to meet her father. His smile was wide.

'Well, Jeff Randall gave his life to God this afternoon.'

Rachel gasped in delight. 'Oh, wow! Do you think he's sincere?'

Her father nodded. 'It certainly seems that way. He's coming to church on Sunday and I've given him a Bible and a few devotional books to read.'

'What about youth group? Is he coming on Friday?'

Rachel's father shook his head. 'No. He sings in a city

nightclub band on Friday and Saturday nights. I didn't even suggest he give it up at this stage. God will lead him in the right time. To tell you the truth, I wonder if he can have more impact for God by being his representative in a scene like that than by avoiding the place.'

Rachel stared at her father in amazement. She had always thought her father was against going into such a place.

He saw her look. 'It's not the place that's the problem, Rachel,' he said quietly. 'It's the human nature expressed there. If Jeff is strong enough not to give in to the temptations presented, that will have more of an impact on people than we can imagine.'

Rachel smiled at her father. Jeff Randall had given his life to God! As she prayed that evening before bed, she added a prayer for Jeff Randall in his new found faith.

***

Rachel arrived at school with a new bounce in her step. God had used her song to bring someone to know and love him. There was no greater joy than to know another person had come to know her best friend as his own.

She watched as Bonnie Blake approached Mr Richardson, the teacher on playground duty that morning, who was also Bonnie's uncle. She threw Rachel a quick wink and Rachel knew entertainment was on its way.

Bonnie tapped the teacher on the shoulder. 'Uncle Bill, Prince Clements is having some trouble.'

Immediately she had Mr Richardson's complete attention. 'What do you mean?'

'Well, he was doing one of his circus tricks and got kind of stuck.'

Mr Richardson followed Bonnie and Rachel wasn't far behind. They arrived to find Prince Clements sitting on the ground, both legs tucked up around his neck. Several students stood around, staring and laughing and Kylie held Prince's schoolbag, impatiently waiting for him to walk to class with her.

Mr Richardson opened and shut his mouth a few times before managing to speak. 'What happened?'

Prince grinned. 'I kind of got stuck.'

'But if you got your legs there can't you get them down?'

Prince frowned in a convincing manner. 'How?'

'Well, can't you kind of … ' Mr Richardson looked at a loss and his expression was too much for Bonnie. She burst into helpless laughter, followed by Prince, who could no longer keep in the position. His legs came down as he rolled on the ground.

Mr Richardson shook his head at his niece. 'You're a tease.' He reached a hand to help Prince up. 'Don't you be led astray by my niece's lack of respect for me, Prince Clements. It will catch up with her one day.'

'I'm sure it will, Mr Richardson,' Prince gave a pleasant smile, 'but you have to admit it's a lot of fun for now.'

Rachel watched with mixed feelings. Prince seemed so perfect in every way. He just hadn't given his life to God and it didn't seem likely he would. She raced to catch up with the impatient Kylie, who had given up waiting for Prince.

CHAPTER SEVEN

A bell rang across the school yard and Rachel looked at Kylie in surprise. 'What's that for?'

Kylie gave a careless shrug. 'Probably to warn us about drunkenness. A few people got a bit plastered at the disco last night.'

Rachel was concerned. She worried every time she heard there was a disco on. She hated the thought of her classmates being drunk and vulnerable. She grabbed her school bag and headed to the assembly area. 'I wish they wouldn't do it.'

Kylie laughed, grabbing her own bag and following Rachel. 'It's not that serious, Rach. It's not life threatening or anything. I don't think you can really judge until you've tried it.'

'Tried alcohol?' Rachel demanded. 'After seeing the effect it has on people? No way!'

'What about just coming to the disco, then?'

'No.'

'Why not?'

'It's not my scene.'

Kylie nodded. 'So you keep saying. But church isn't my scene and you keep asking me to come. How can you expect anyone to consider your lifestyle if you haven't even tried mine? How can you really know yours is better?'

'I can just tell. Some things are obvious.' She met Kylie's challenging look. 'Jeff Randall can see it. He became a Christian yesterday.'

Kylie's eyes widened in interest, then she smiled. 'See, that just proves my point.'

'It does? How?'

'Well, Jeff can relate to you and your lifestyle because he's a musician like you. When you sang that song at assembly, you were speaking his language. If you come to a disco, then you'll be speaking *our* language.'

Rachel studied her cousin doubtfully as they arrived in the assembly area and lined up. 'All right,' she conceded. 'I'll come to the next disco, but I won't drink.'

'Fine.' Kylie shot her a triumphant smile. 'I'll hold you to it, Rachel Seton!'

Rachel looked up expectantly at the principal standing before the school about to make an announcement. However, her mind was on her promise to Kylie. What had she let herself in for?

The principal's discerning eyes scanned the students gathered on the school lawn. His piercing gaze had even the innocent squirming. 'Some of you may have noticed the police officers here this morning.' His voice came out hard and raspy. 'And those who didn't notice are sure to have heard about them.'

There was dry humour in the comment but Rachel was too tense to appreciate it. 'It seems that some foolish teenagers in this town have decided it might be fun to do a bit of surfing. Don't get me wrong – I have nothing against surfing when there are waves and surf boards involved. But sliding around on the top of a car or in the back of a ute is just asking to die young.'

Those eyes glared around again, falling hard on a year seven student who had found the whole situation amusing until that moment.

The principal looked around slowly and deliberately. 'Now we have a fair idea who is involved and we will be keeping a close eye on you so that if you do it again you can expect to be caught, because you will be. Now go to class.'

It took a few moments before the group began to shuffle and gather their belongings and head off to class. It was a full minute before anyone spoke.

Brad Jenson kicked a piece of rubbish along the ground. 'All that just for a warning about something that didn't even happen in school hours? What a waste of time.'

Bonnie Blake chuckled at him. 'Too right. You could have copied down half of my Maths homework by now!'

Brad ignored her comment, but seemed irritated. Rachel wondered if his own father scared him. He kept up his complaint.

'As if car surfing has killed or injured more people than hooning around in one has.'

Bonnie laughed at him. 'You're just upset that your father told us all off. You'd be a whole lot less scared of car surfing if my uncle had been the one standing up there today. You can ignore the deputy principal, but you can't ignore your own father, can you?'

Brad glared at her in an unsuccessful attempt to silence her all too knowing words.

'You just don't like being told what to do, Brad Jenson!'

He gave a wry smile. 'That's because I don't need to be told.'

'No, it's because you're too arrogant to recognise that you don't know it all.'

He stopped short and stood a little taller. 'What don't I know? Come on, ask me anything!'

Rachel grinned at the ridiculous challenge but Bonnie didn't let it go.

'Okay then.' She raised her wide blue eyes to the sky as if deep in thought, then looked hard at Brad. 'Who was car surfing?'

There was silence for a few moments, then Brad slowly shook his head. 'No way, Bonnie Blake. I'm not going to dob myself in.'

'You just did.'

'I didn't. I didn't say who or what and if you're going to take me out of context –'

'Come on, Brad. Just give me one name.'

'Why?'

She shrugged. 'Because I just want to know.'

'But why?'

Bonnie looked sheepish. 'Because I'm looking for adventure.'

Brad's expression was shocked, then determined. 'No way, Bonnie Blake. There is no way I'd let you –' He stopped short, as though realising he was about to say more than he should. He gave Bonnie an annoyed look and began to walk away. Bonnie danced along at his elbow, stopping his progress.

'What if I blackmail you?'

'You've got no evidence to blackmail me with.'

'I could easily find some.'

Brad swore and turned his back on her as he raced off to class. Rachel grinned, knowing Bonnie would never tell anyone about Brad's car surfing. She liked to hassle him but she wouldn't cause him trouble.

CHAPTER EIGHT

'Where's Bonnie Blake this morning?' Miss Sanders asked her class as students took their seats early Monday morning.

'Didn't you hear?' Belinda's voice was full of anguish. 'It was in today's newspaper.'

Rachel felt her heart begin to thump in her chest. Surely something hadn't happened to the lively, carefree Bonnie?

'No, what happened?'

Sarah May was the one to answer. 'She was in a fire on Friday afternoon and got burned. That's why Mr Richardson and the Clements aren't here. It was a fire at the Clements' horse stables.'

Miss Sanders' face paled. 'How bad? Is she badly burned?'

'Pretty bad.'

'But she'll be okay?'

Belinda nodded. 'It was touch and go all weekend but now they're saying she should pull through. She's still in a coma, though.'

Rachel said nothing but she felt sick. Bonnie Blake could have died and she, Rachel Seton had never done anything to try to tell her about Jesus. It was true she had prayed for her, just as she prayed for all her classmates, but was prayer without actions enough? She decided that, given another chance, she would do her best to share her faith with the popular Bonnie.

Kylie pulled a newspaper out of her schoolbag at lunchtime. 'Have you seen it?'

Rachel gasped at the picture of the attractive Bonnie Blake now horribly burned and unconscious. Quickly she began to read the article. A man from the Clements' circus had attempted to steal their horses and had set the stables on fire. Bonnie had been burned trying to rescue one of the horses.

Kylie was staring at the picture. 'Prince said Blaze is pretty cut up about it. He was getting close to Bonnie.'

Rachel's throat felt dry. 'I can't believe it. She looks terrible!'

'I know. It's so sad,' Kylie agreed. 'I thought Bonnie Blake finally found herself a guy she could love instead of compete with and now this.'

Rachel looked at her cousin in genuine surprise. 'How does this change anything between her and Blaze?'

'Well, you saw her. She's all burned. It's sickening to look at.'

Anger began to build inside Rachel. She glared at her cousin. 'I don't think Blaze was just attracted to her looks. There's a whole lot more to Bonnie than her looks and perfect figure.'

Kylie laughed. 'Rachel, when are you going to live in reality and see people for what they really are? It's my bet that Bonnie has seen the end of Blaze Clements. I know he's a Christian and all that but he's human.'

'I think you're wrong. He'll stick by her.'

Kylie shrugged. 'Fine. You go ahead and dream the world is a perfect place and that people are ultimately good, but remember I tried to warn you.'

***

Class seemed quiet without Bonnie, and even Brad seemed sombre. Prince's absence meant Kylie went back to sitting with Rachel but Rachel wished she wouldn't. Kylie had changed since she had fallen in love with the charming circus performer. She no longer spent much time with Rachel and she was closed and distant. Rachel suspected the two had become intimate and that Kylie knew her actions would disappoint and grieve her.

Rachel would never bring the subject up and so could never be sure, however, the public physical connection between the two suggested there was a lot more than kissing going on in private.

As soon as Rachel arrived home, she sought out her father who was preparing a sermon in his office. 'Have you heard about Bonnie Blake?'

Nodding, her father picked up the newspaper from where it lay on his desk. 'I read about it. And I've prayed for her.'

'But you haven't seen Bonnie?'

'No. I believe she's still unconscious in one of the city hospitals.'

Rachel sighed as she sat in the chair in front of her father's desk. 'She nearly died, Dad.' Her eyes welled with tears. 'And I've never told her about Jesus – about life after death. What if she dies before she gets a chance to know him? Sometimes I get so carried away with the now I forget about eternity and what's really important.'

Her father said nothing as he studied her worried frown.

Suddenly Rachel sat up. 'Dad, do you think it's enough to just pray for someone to know God?'

Her father rubbed his chin, eyes thoughtful. 'I don't know. I know some people have a gift of sharing their faith and convincing others of its truth. Others are better at praying. But I believe if we're serious about God we should do both.'

'So if I pray someone will become a Christian but do nothing about it, God won't answer that prayer?'

Her father looked thoughtful. 'I wouldn't say that. After all, God can do anything. He doesn't need us. And I don't think someone would go to hell just because I failed to say something I should have. Witnessing is a lot more than words, Rachel. I think prayer, actions, faith, all those things are involved. It's about a whole lifestyle – who we are. When we live with hope and purpose in a world where most people are feeling despair, they will soon recognise we have a God worth knowing and living for.'

Rachel nodded, then met her father's eyes. 'Dad, will you please go and visit Bonnie and her parents? I know it's a long way to the city hospital, but they must really need support right now.' As Rachel spoke, a knock came at the office door. Mrs Seton poked her head in.

'Mike, Blaze Clements is here.'

Rachel's father nodded. 'Send him in.'

Rachel looked for an escape but Blaze was blocking the doorway.

'Mr Seton, Rachel.' Blaze acknowledged, then without even sitting down, went on. 'Mr Seton, I guess you've heard all about the fire? Well I was just wondering if you could maybe go and visit Bonnie and her parents. Her parents are taking it very hard, and well, I haven't been a Christian for long, and I don't know what to say. And I have no way of getting there on my own, anyway.'

Mr Seton stood with a smile. 'Rachel was just asking me to do the same thing.'

Blaze glanced at Rachel with a grateful look, then back to her father. 'So will you?'

Mr Seton nodded. 'I will. I'll just let my wife know and we'll be on our way.'

Rachel watched as her father stood and headed out the door with Blaze, snatching up his wallet and car keys on the way. Slowly she sat down in her father's empty office and began to pray. This time she prayed not only for Blaze, Bonnie and her father, but also for Prince Clements and Kylie. With all her heart she longed for them to know God.

***

'Bonnie is in a bad way,' Rachel's father admitted when he finally arrived home. 'She's still unconscious but it's expected she'll pull through.'

'And her parents?' Rachel's mother handed baby Paul to her husband, whose eyes took on a glow.

'They were touched that I came and prayed for her. They've asked me back again. They were asking me all sorts of questions about God.'

51

'Did you invite them to church?'

'Yes, and they said they'd come when they get back home. Blaze said he would, too. We had a good talk about the need for fellowship. That boy's amazing.'

Rachel's ears pricked up. 'Amazing how?'

'He's never belonged to a church or been taught by anyone else who knows God, he just reads theology books. And he's determined to become a minister.'

'So how did he come to believe?'

'Apparently he met a Christian one night when he was still in the circus and she told him about Jesus. He gave his life to God that night.'

Rachel's mother took back baby Paul who was beginning to fuss. 'God must have been working in him before that, though.'

Mr Seton nodded. 'He was. Blaze had been searching for a while. He knew there was more to life and had been looking into all kinds of beliefs. God had claimed him way before the girl ever spoke to him that night.'

Rachel frowned, then swallowed hard. 'What do you think would have happened if that girl never spoke to him?'

'God would have sent someone else.' Rachel's father sounded confident and she was relieved. But in her heart she was aching to help her friends, to do more than sing and pray.

***

Sleep didn't come easily for Rachel that night. Visions of Bonnie Blake, Jeff Randall's cousin and Prince Clements kept swimming before her eyes. She knew she had to tell them about God. If she didn't, who would? She felt so burdened she knew that if she were standing before them that moment she would beg them on her knees with heart-felt tears to turn to God. She would pour out her heart as she never had before, imploring them with the love of God to make peace with him.

However, in the morning the intensity of that feeling had gone and was once more replaced with fear and feelings of inadequacy. Only the memory of the night before remained. Getting out a pen, Rachel knew she had to capture the memory before it faded altogether. Thinking of the awful fire that almost consumed Bonnie and that could have stolen the lives of the Clements family members, Rachel began to write:

I burned ablaze with fear last night
for you and for your soul,
But this morning stole the fire
which yearned to see you whole.

I know the burdens were not mine
for fickle is my heart
It could never dream up hurts
that tore me so apart.

So in morning light I see
my fire has now gone out
The source remains, reminding me
God loves you without doubt.

All this love I have for you,
each burden that I feel
Is coming from the Prince of Peace
whose love I can't conceal.

Rachel read back over what she had written.

'Whose love I can't conceal?' She shook her head as she read the last line. Even as she took the poem and put it in her schoolbag, she knew she would never have the courage to give it to Prince or Bonnie.

CHAPTER NINE

Rachel couldn't enjoy the general conversation of her classmates. Things weren't the same without Bonnie around. Belinda was now disruptive and often thrown out of class. Rachel suspected she was trying to make up for Bonnie's absence. Belinda also took on the responsibility of heckling Brad Jenson. But there was a big difference between Bonnie Blake and Belinda. For a start, Belinda was far more interested in the male population than Bonnie ever had been.

'Jeff Randall is hot,' Belinda told the class with a coy smile as she gave each male a rating out of ten. 'But he doesn't know it.'

'I think he does know it,' Sarah May said. 'That's why he's not chasing any girls. He knows they'll come to him.'

'I'm telling you, he's gay!' Brad shouted from across the room. 'That's why he sings and does all those girlie things.'

Belinda gave Brad the disgusted look Bonnie had always saved just for him and threw a banana peel in his direction. 'You are so uncultured! I suppose you think Elvis was gay? And the Beatles? And every male who happens to have a gift that you don't?'

'Defending Jeff are you?' Brad shot back. 'Are you interested in him?'

'Of course not! I like a challenge. Jeff is too, well, too nice.'

'Hah!' Brad grinned triumphantly. 'And making a gay guy straight isn't enough of a challenge for you?'

It was at that point that Jeff himself entered the room and all fell silent.

'Who's gay?' When no one answered, Jeff glanced around at the awkward expressions surrounding him and left the room again without another word.

'Oops,' Belinda said quietly when he was out of earshot.

Brad shrugged. 'He didn't deny it.'

'We didn't give him a chance, you narrow minded wind bag!' Belinda said angrily. 'We didn't even have the decency to confess we were talking about him.'

'He knew, though,' Brad said. 'As soon as he heard the word "gay" he knew we were talking about him.'

Rachel felt anger burn within her until it burst out and she had to speak. 'Only because he knows what you're like!'

'Meaning?' Brad's expression was dangerous. Rachel didn't blink. She had to speak now or she never would.

'Meaning you stereotype people and jump to conclusions without knowing any facts. The rumours you start and spread are so totally unfair. Jeff isn't stupid. As if he didn't work out you were talking about him!'

Brad had now broken into a grin and he let out a hoot. 'Rachel likes a gay guy! How ironic! Religious Rachel's in love with Jeff!'

'Shut up!' Sarah May cut him off and soon the room echoed her sentiment.

Rachel hoped no one saw her blushing as she left and headed to the music room. Jeff had started coming to church and had been spending time with her father to learn about the Christian faith. Jeff was Rachel's reason for hope. If someone like Jeff Randall could become a Christian, there were endless possibilities.

Rachel found Jeff alone at the piano, staring at the music book. She lowered herself beside him and raised tentative eyes to his. 'What are you doing?'

He turned and she saw the sorrow written on his face. 'I have the wrong gift.'

'Wrong gift?'

'Yeah. I should be out there playing football, building houses, looking at motorbikes or something like that. Instead I'm in here writing songs. Like you.'

His suffering renewed Rachel's confidence. She couldn't bear to see anybody in pain. 'Music is not a girl's gift,' she said firmly. 'They all know that. It's just Brad.'

'Brad,' Jeff agreed with a sigh. 'Brad the footballer, the tough guy, the principal's son. Whatever he says goes.'

'Not always. They were all standing up for you in there. And Belinda nearly got Brad in the face with a banana peel.'

Jeff nearly smiled. 'But they still think I'm gay.'

'I don't think most of them do. And I definitely don't.' Rachel was surprised at her own words. Something had happened last night to give her a confidence she had never had before.

'You don't?'

Rachel shook her head. 'No. And I like you the way you are. Your gift makes you special.'

'But not masculine.'

Rachel stared, then laughed. 'Jeff, there's nothing feminine about you! They all presume you're homosexual because you're so good looking but don't have a girlfriend.'

'That's it?' His eyes bored into hers.

'That's it. That's how narrow minded they are.'

Jeff stood for a moment, his eyes still fixed on Rachel's. She flamed red under his gaze and looked away until she felt strong fingers entwine with hers. Her eyes flew back to his.

'Is this okay?'

Rachel's heart hammered in her chest. 'Um, I guess so.'

He pulled her down onto the piano seat beside him and looked deep into her eyes. 'Have you ever had a boyfriend?'

She shook her head, speechless, her head spinning. Where

was this headed? Was the gifted, reserved Jeff Randell interested in her? As a girlfriend? He was a believer, so there was nothing stopping her from being open to it.

He drew her hand to his lap. 'There's something different about you today, Rachel. Or am I just seeing you differently now that I'm a Christian?'

'I don't know.' Rachel gazed up at him. Why hadn't she noticed the depths of his eyes before? She had palmed him off as good looking and therefore arrogant but she now knew she had made a mistake.

'Rachel, I've never had a girlfriend before.' His tone implored her to believe his words, to take him seriously. 'Not because I didn't want one but just because I never found the right one. I think I've just found the right one. Will you have me?'

Just like that? Rachel didn't know what to think. But he seemed so earnest. He had to be genuine.

She nodded, her face filling with familiar warmth and he chuckled.

'Do you think we'll ever get to a point where you will feel comfortable talking to me and stop blushing every time I look in your direction?'

Rachel bit her lip. 'I hope so.'

He ran a hand down her cheek. 'We'll work on it.'

He made it sound like a promise she wanted him to keep.

***

Rachel made the effort to visit Kylie that afternoon. Prince still hadn't returned to school and Kylie was bored. The two chatted for a while, then Rachel knew she must tell her cousin about Jeff.

'Kylie?'

'Yeah?'

'I have a boyfriend. It's Jeff.' There. It was said, plain and simple.

57

'Pardon?"
'Jeff and I ...'
Kylie stared. 'You're kidding!'
'No.'
'Then why didn't you say so? Today, when everyone was saying stuff about him?'
'He asked me after that.'
Kylie was stunned speechless, then her eyes took on a new light. 'I told you! I told you that one day a guy would see you for who you really are but I never imagined Jeff! I'm envious. He's hot! And his voice is unbelievable! Rachel, you've just got to hear him sing!'
Rachel stared. What about Prince? Was Kylie really that fickle? Maybe Kylie didn't really care for Prince. Maybe she just cared about whoever was there in the moment.

***

Kylie took a day off school to visit the Clements family. Rachel wished she had the courage to go with her but instead trudged off to school and sat in her normal seat in class, expecting to be alone.
'How's it going?'
Rachel turned at the sound of the deep voice now becoming familiar. Jeff approached, his eyes alight with friendliness.
'Okay,' she gave a shy smile, wishing her heart would slow down so she could think. It stubbornly thumped away in her chest.
'Kylie's not here today?'
'No.'
Jeff grinned at her short, awkward answers and sat himself beside her. 'I see we haven't got the talking thing perfected yet.'
She felt her face becoming warm. Jeff had never sat next to her in class before and other students were turning to stare at them.
'What?' Jeff gave them an even look as he leaned back comfortably in his chair.
Brad screwed up his nose in scorn. 'She's female, that's what.'

58

'As if I hadn't noticed.' Mouths dropped open as Jeff put an arm around Rachel and drew her against him.

'So you two are an item?'

'You could say that.'

'But she's religious.'

Jeff's cool gaze met Brad's. 'You'd be surprised what I believe, Brad Jenson.'

Brad was stunned into silence and the class was forced to turn to the front as the teacher arrived.

'Ready for work?' The teacher's question received the usual groan.

'Can't we play football today?' Brad whined. 'We'll take turns scoring. It will improve our Maths.'

The teacher didn't even bother to answer but glanced in surprise at Jeff and Rachel sitting so close together. Rachel subtly moved away and Jeff grinned at her. 'Too close?'

'No. I just couldn't concentrate on Maths.'

He nodded and let her have her space.

CHAPTER TEN

'Rachel, we want to speak with you.'

Rachel looked at her parents' serious expressions and felt her heart tighten in her chest. Paul had finally settled to sleep and the house was quiet again. Her parents sat side by side on the lounge, holding hands.

'We are thinking of going to visit Grandpa Seton but wanted to discuss it with you first.'

'Is that all?' Rachel gave a sigh of relief. Nothing was seriously wrong. She thought of her grandfather who was a missionary in the Hanoa Strait Islands. 'You mean you're going to the Islands?'

'Yes, but we were thinking it's best not to take you with us, not with your exams coming up.'

Rachel nodded as she sat across from them. 'What about Paul?'

'Well, he's the main reason we're thinking of going. Grandpa is going through a bit of a tough time and we thought meeting Paul might cheer him up.'

Rachel watched the way her parents glanced at one another meaningfully and waited.

'Rachel, there have been a lot of problems in the islands lately. It could be dangerous.'

She tried not to look alarmed. 'Meaning?'

'Well, we trust God for protection but we can't guarantee we'll come home.'

'So why are you thinking of going? If you could be risking your lives and Paul's.' Even as she spoke the words, she knew why her parents were going. They believed God had asked them to. Besides, it was hard for her father to know his father was struggling alone on the island without any family nearby.

Shrugging, she moved to the lounge her parents were on and snuggled up against her father, reaching for her mother's hand at the same time. 'I don't believe God will take you yet. You've got too much work left to do. So go with my blessing and prayers.'

Her parents smiled at one another and Rachel pulled back from her father's embrace. 'So what about me? Do I get to stay here on my own?'

Her father laughed. 'Wishful thinking! No, especially not now that you have a boyfriend. We've asked Grandma and Grandpa Blythe to come and stay with you while we're away.'

Rachel's face softened as she thought of her mother's parents. They lived an hour away but she had seen them often since the birth of baby Paul. She loved them dearly and had often wished she could be as close to her missionary grandfather.

So it was arranged. Within a few weeks, her parents would leave for the Hanoa Islands and she, Rachel, would be left home to study.

***

'My parents are going to the Hanoa Strait Islands for a while,' Rachel told Jeff as he said goodbye for the weekend.

'And you're not going?'

'No. I'm staying home.'

'Alone?' Jeff's look was strange.

'No. My grandparents are coming to stay.' Rachel wondered at the relief she saw in Jeff's expression. She put it down to concern for her. He didn't want her to be lonely.

Somehow having a boyfriend gave Rachel confidence. True, she didn't spend a lot of time with Jeff but she now felt free to be friends with other males. She didn't need to fear giving the impression she was attracted to them. They would know she wasn't; she had a boyfriend. They could accept her friendship for what it was.

Kylie was suddenly at her door, gazing after Jeff. 'He's off again? Not a very attentive boyfriend, is he? I hardly ever see him.'

Rachel didn't ask her cousin why she should expect to see her boyfriend when she had one of her own. Instead, she shrugged. 'He's singing at another nightclub tonight and tomorrow night. He has to practice with the band.'

'Why don't you go with him?'

'Ky, you know it's not my scene.'

Kylie gave a wicked grin. 'Not yet. But the school disco is in a few days and I'm holding you to your promise! I expect you to come.'

Rachel groaned. 'You don't need me to come with you. You've got Prince and I'll just be in the way.'

Kylie stretched out on Rachel's floor and kicked carelessly at Rachel's schoolbag lying there. 'Prince and I are having a fight.'

'Another one?' Rachel hadn't meant the words to come out the way they did but it bothered her how fragile Kylie and Prince's relationship seemed to be.

'Well at least I see him sometimes!' Kylie became defensive. 'At least we *touch* each other!'

Rachel frowned at the pointed comment, hoping to change the subject. But Kylie was on a roll.

'Have you and Jeff ever even kissed?'

'No.'

'Why not?'

'I'm not ready for it.' She picked up her hairbrush and began working on her long, blonde hair.

'But Rachel, it's been two months. Are you sure he's not gay?'

Rachel slammed down her brush in disgust. 'You have a one track mind, Kylie Sandom! Of course I'm sure. He's my boyfriend for goodness' sake. Just because we have standards and don't sleep together doesn't make him homosexual, me either, for that matter.'

Kylie opened her mouth in shock, then a look of hurt passed over her face. 'I wasn't saying you were.'

Immediately, Rachel was sorry. 'I know you weren't. I'm just sensitive at the moment.'

Kylie looked apologetic. 'I guess I am, too. Come on Rachel, let's not talk about boyfriends.'

Gratefully, Rachel agreed.

Kylie glanced around the room then to the door. 'I'm bored. What can we do?'

Rachel thought back to the money her parents had given her to buy new clothes. She hadn't bought any yet. Once Jeff had asked her out, it suddenly hadn't seemed to matter as much how she looked. But now she had the disco coming up and she had no idea what to wear.

'We could go shopping.'

Kylie looked surprised. 'What for?'

'Clothes.'

'I don't need any.'

'No, but I do. I've got some money put away but I don't want to go shopping on my own.'

'Well why didn't you say?' Kylie jumped up with a grin. 'Quick, grab your money, let's go!'

Rachel laughed at Kylie's enthusiasm and followed her cousin out the door. 'Mum, we're going shopping!' She stopped short, realising her mother was trying to get the unsettled baby Paul to sleep. She changed her voice to a whisper. 'Oops, sorry.'

Her mother waved a hand and smiled. 'Don't worry about it. Have fun.'

But Rachel had noticed how weary her mother looked. 'Perhaps I should stay. I could give you a break.'

'No! You go. We're fine. Look, he's almost asleep.'

Hesitantly, Rachel followed the impatient Kylie out the door. The moment they were out of the house, Kylie turned on her.

'What were you thinking? You nearly got us stuck back there looking after the baby.'

Rachel shrugged, knowing Kylie wouldn't understand her concern for her mother. Trying to put her mother's tired eyes from her mind, she walked beside Kylie to the shopping centre. Kylie's taste was a lot more adventurous than Rachel's, but finally they agreed on a compromise and Rachel came home a few hours later, feeling satisfied with who she was and how she looked.

Then she saw her mother's tiredness again.

'You go and lie down for a while,' she suggested. 'I can entertain Paul and get the tea on.'

Gratefully, her mother went to get some rest. Rachel took little Paul and sat him in the bouncer while she peeled some potatoes. His smile was content as he watched her, and knowing her parents would be taking him to the Hanoa Strait islands in a few weeks, Rachel determined to make the most of the time she had with him.

CHAPTER ELEVEN

The school disco was in full swing with lights flashing and music blaring. Rachel glanced around the crowded dance floor, trying to spot Kylie. Why had she promised her cousin she would come? Wasn't anybody else bothered by the deafening noise and blinding lights? Maybe she just needed to get used to the atmosphere. Then again, maybe she should escape while she could. Kylie wouldn't miss her. She had left her side the moment they arrived and for the past half hour Rachel had been trying to stop her hands shaking. She had given up trying to talk to anyone anymore. They couldn't hear her above the music, anyway, so she just hung around trying to look occupied and involved.

'How are you going?'

Finally! Kylie had returned. Rachel shouted back into her ear, 'I've got a bit of a headache.'

'What? You'll have to speak louder.'

Rachel just shrugged, unwilling to raise her voice again. Her throat was tired from trying to make herself heard. She'd had enough.

'A few of us are heading to the park,' Kylie shouted above the music. 'Want to come?'

Rachel nodded. Some silence and fresh air was exactly what she needed. Kylie disappeared again but Rachel saw a group of teenagers heading out the door and knew they were the ones to follow.

'Never thought I'd see *you* here.'

Rachel turned to see Bonnie Blake's friend, Belinda, and smiled. 'Me either.'

'So what made you come? Bored with the ol' Christian way of life?'

'No. Kylie challenged me to not make judgements on her lifestyle until I tried it for myself.'

Belinda laughed in genuine amusement. 'And have you?'

'Made judgements?'

'No. Tried her lifestyle.'

Rachel shrugged. 'Yeah, I guess I have, now.'

'What do you think?'

Rachel hesitated, not wanting to offend the popular girl but unwilling to openly speak her mind. 'I think it's not for me. I've ended up with a bit of a headache.'

Belinda laughed again. 'You always do, first time. But then you kind of desensitise.'

Rachel nodded, then frowned. 'I don't really like not being able to hear people or be heard, either.'

'But that's the good thing about loud music!' Belinda assured her. 'Nobody can hear the stupid things you say so you can get as drunk as you like, say whatever you like and do whatever you want to. It helps you lighten up a bit.'

Belinda looked hard at Rachel, then. 'I'm surprised you haven't relaxed a bit. How much have you had?'

'How much what?'

'Diet coke. What do you think?'

'Alcohol? None.'

'None? You're kidding me! Then how can you really know what this is all about?'

Suddenly Brad Jenson was there, waving a beer can under her nose. 'Yeah, that's right. How can you know?'

The beer sloshed on Rachel's skirt and she backed away.

'Drink it, God-girl!' Brad forced the can toward her mouth

and Rachel pushed it away. She reached for the mobile phone in her pocket. It was obviously time to head home. However, Brad saw what she was doing and snatched the phone from her hand. He called to his friend Jez, and threw it to him. Jez was less drunk than Brad, and caught it neatly. The two threw it back and forward tauntingly, while frustrated, Rachel watched them, knowing it wasn't worth trying to retrieve it. She would have to wait until they grew bored and gave it back. But then, Prince Clements stepped forward and neatly intercepted the phone before Brad or Jez even saw him coming.

'Come on, guys. You've had your fun. Time to give it back.'

'Why?' Brad made a useless grab at the phone. 'So she can ring her Preacher Daddy and ask him to come and rescue her from us bad boys?'

Prince said nothing as he handed the phone to Rachel. Brad moved closer, breathing alcohol fumes into Prince's face. 'Is that it, Clements?'

Prince screwed up his face and stepped back, provoking Brad to further aggression.

'Is that it, coward?' He pushed Prince in the chest.

Prince stood his ground. 'No and I'm not a coward.'

Brad's expression became a sneer. 'Prove it.'

Prince took the challenge. 'You tell me how and I'll prove it.'

Brad laughed an ugly laugh as he turned to Jez. 'What about a bit of the forbidden car surfing, Jez? Me and you and the royalty here.'

Jez looked smug. 'Sounds good to me. What speed?'

Brad frowned as though deep in thought, then waved his beer can in the air. 'What the heck? How about a hundred?'

'A hundred?' Belinda echoed in a whisper and those in the crowd shook their heads.

'Don't be stupid,' someone called, but Prince looked unconcerned.

'You're on.' He headed toward Jez's ute. The crowd followed.

Fear seized Rachel's heart as she raced after them. *They think they're invincible!* Suddenly Brad stopped and turned on her. He came up close until she felt his breath on her cheek. 'Don't you dare tell anyone, God-girl,' he hissed, 'or you'll be sorry.'

Prince was now standing on the back of the ute. 'Leave her alone. Your fight is with me, now.'

'Don't do it!' Rachel pleaded. 'Didn't Bonnie Blake's accident teach you anything?'

Brad laughed. 'Yeah. Never run into a burning stable.'

'That's exactly what you're doing!'

'Huh?' Brad screwed up his nose in confusion.

'It's poetic,' Prince explained and Brad laughed.

'That's right. I forgot she's the poem lady. Just one friend …'

Rachel blushed deep red and Prince glanced her way. 'Leave her alone.' He looked away. 'Let's get going.'

'Prince,' Rachel pleaded, but the ute had screamed off around the corner and into the dark night, Prince easily keeping his balance even as the ute swayed from side to side. She just caught a glimpse of him climbing from the back onto the roof and heard all the spectators gasp.

Rachel turned away, her heart in her throat as she begged God to protect Prince. There was nothing she could do now and so with a heavy heart she called her father to come and pick her up.

'How did it go?' Her father leaned across the passenger seat to open the door for her. She climbed in beside him. Her pale, unhappy face answered for her as she remembered her father's words that afternoon.

'It's true we're to be in the world but not of it,' he had told her, 'but we have to work out at what point we are compromising our safety and our faith.'

She let out a heavy sigh. 'I didn't get caught up in anything, but I'm so worried about some of them. They're doing illegal stuff but if I dob them in, they'll never talk to me again.'

'Illegal things?' Now she had his complete attention. He slowed the car down and looked over at her. 'Are they putting lives at risk?'

With tears, Rachel nodded, then heard herself gasp when up ahead she saw flashing lights. Had her fear of what people thought failed her to stop a terrible tragedy? If Prince was hurt, she'd never forgive herself.

Her father pulled the car over to the side of the road. A police car was parked behind Jez's ute, and two police officers were speaking to Jez and Brad. Prince was nowhere to be seen. Rachel didn't know whether to be relieved or concerned.

'Drink driving, no doubt,' her father said and Rachel nodded.

'And car surfing, too. Blaze's brother was involved.'

Her father's brows rose. 'Kylie's boyfriend? Should I be warning Kylie's parents?'

Rachel shook her head. 'Kylie's safe. They broke up.'

Her father got out and spoke to the officers, then came back to the car. 'They're all fine. Just in a bit of trouble.'

All night, Rachel struggled in prayer. Baby Paul was unsettled and cried throughout the night until finally morning arrived. Tiredness left hollow rings beneath Rachel's eyes, but her mother didn't seem to notice. She had tiredness of her own to deal with.

Rachel didn't have to ask after Prince. Everyone at school was talking about him.

'He didn't even fall off!' some were saying in admiration, while others were less impressed.

Even Kylie seemed disgusted with Prince. 'When the police came he took off, leaving Brad and Jez to take the rap.' She screwed up her pretty nose. 'Everyone knows it was Prince but he denies it and he wasn't there when the police got there so there's no proof.'

Rachel was concerned. 'How's Brad taking it?'

'He hates Prince now. And no wonder!'

Rachel wondered why everyone was upset with Prince. It

was Brad and Jez who had challenged him to car surf in the first place. In a way he had done it to get them to leave her alone.

Kylie's eyes lit up. 'So what did you think of the disco?'

Rachel turned away. 'I can't speak that language, Kylie. In fact, I can't even speak or hear when the music is so loud. I'll have to find another way to relate to our classmates.'

'I didn't think you would fit,' Kylie acknowledged. 'Just like no one here would fit in your church scene.'

Rachel watched as Kylie then bounced off to class. She wondered if there was anywhere she did fit. It seemed she was one of those people who sat on the sidelines and prayed for people. Her influence the night before was non-existent - even negative – and she might as well have stayed home. However, perhaps her prayers had saved Prince Clements from injury, even death. From now on, she would just watch and pray.

Despite Kylie declaring she had 'dropped' Prince because of his unsportsmanlike behaviour with Brad and Jez, she still vied for his attention at every opportunity. Rachel watched with wry amusement and concern. She knew the fight between the two was not destined to last. Kylie always got what she wanted and it was clear despite her words that she still wanted Prince Clements.

CHAPTER TWELVE

'Bonnie Blake is back!'

Rachel heard the students talking as she came in the school gate. Her heart beat faster. If she was serious about wanting Bonnie to know God, she needed to make an effort to speak to her. However, when she first set eyes on Bonnie that morning, she was stunned into silence. The wide blue eyes that had once sparkled with life now held a haunted, pained look. That perfect figure now displayed wrinkled, shrivelled skin which Bonnie was obviously trying to hide beneath the burn garment and gloves she wore.

'She looks horrible!' Kylie whispered to Rachel. Rachel glared, knowing it was true but thinking it didn't need to be said.

In class, Bonnie sat silently, no longer calling out and causing mischief as she once did. And when Brad Jenson made ridiculous comments, Bonnie didn't even seem to notice. It wasn't long before the students had chosen a new nickname for the once popular girl.

'Frankenstein,' they called her, and Rachel listened, aghast. She couldn't believe how fickle people were. Couldn't they see past the burns and recognise that Bonnie Blake was still the same person? Did people really judge each other so much by outward appearance?

Rachel didn't see Bonnie again after that first day at school. It was rumoured she and her parents had left town. Deeply concerned, Rachel continued her earnest prayer that someday, somehow, Bonnie Blake would come to know God and that he would help heal her physically and emotionally from all she had been through in the fire.

Prince and Kylie quickly recovered from their fight, just as Rachel had predicted, although many other students were still siding with Brad after the car surfing incident. Rachel tried not to notice as Prince stood with his arms around Kylie. He looked so comfortable with her. That is, until his sister, Beauty headed their way. Kylie avoided her eyes but Beauty obviously didn't like being ignored.

'Watch out, Kylie,' the younger girl called over her shoulder as she walked past. 'You might end up carrying another one of Prince's babies.'

Rachel saw the shock that passed over Kylie's face and the anger in Prince's.

'Ignore her.' His voice came out gruff and Kylie spun in his arms to face him.

'Ignore her?' She pushed back from him but left her hands resting on his shoulders. 'That's pretty hard to ignore. Is it true? Do you have a child?'

'Of course not.'

'Then she's going to get it, the little cat.'

'Leave her alone.' Prince's tone was surprisingly firm and Kylie stared at him.

'What?' she demanded. 'Why?'

'Because she's my sister.'

'And you would let her begin rumours like that without doing anything about it?'

Prince said nothing and Kylie's eyes widened 'It's true, isn't it?' Her voice came out low and muffled. 'You have a child.'

'Drop it, Kylie.' Prince was looking anywhere but at her. 'I told you it's not true.'

'I don't believe you.'

'Then there's not much I can do. If you choose to believe my sister over me, that's your choice.'

With that, Prince firmly lifted Kylie's hands from where they rested on his shoulders and headed to the study. Rachel knew it wouldn't be long before word got out. Belinda and Sarah May were the first to rush to Kylie.

'What happened?'

Kylie was now swiping at tears. 'Beauty said Prince got a girl pregnant.'

Belinda shook her head in disgust. 'And you'd believe that little cat?'

Sarah May suddenly looked awkward.

'What?' Kylie demanded. 'Do you know something? Tell me!'

'Tell you what?'

Kylie stared Sarah May down. 'You knew? Prince really has a child?'

Sarah May shrugged. 'I heard the rumour. Blaze told Bonnie about it.'

Kylie was furious with Prince and the girls took her side. They began planning revenge on him. Rachel shook her head as she listened to them from the sidelines. Only days ago Prince was the one these girls were trying to impress. She walked away, not wanting to be part of whatever they were planning. Jeff had booked the music room so she wasn't quite sure what to do. She wandered out into the schoolyard. Then she saw Prince. He sat alone, watching a group of year seven students play handball. The ball rolled away and then the students began a search.

One of them approached Rachel. 'Have you seen the ball?'

Rachel glanced quickly around. 'No, sorry.'

The puzzled student shrugged and then began looking in the bushes surrounding the play area. Rachel thought about joining the search but instead came to Prince and sat beside him. When he turned to look at her, she could barely contain her laughter. His eyes were sparkling with mischief and his mouth was swollen in the shape of a tennis ball.

'I won't bother saying hello,' she told him. 'I can see you can't respond, anyway.'

He almost laughed but had to contain it as a girl searching for the ball headed their way.

'Prince, have you seen –' She stopped short as Prince spat the ball into his hand. He held it out to the girl. She squealed.

'Yuck! Prince Clements, you are so disgusting. I'm not going to touch that slobbery thing!'

Prince shrugged and wiped it down his shirt before holding it out again. 'Here.'

Shaking her head, the girl backed away from Prince. Slowly he followed, unable to suppress his grin. The girl ran from him, so with a shrug, he turned and headed back to Rachel.

'They don't seem to want it anymore.'

Rachel couldn't suppress her giggle. 'I'm not surprised.'

'Why? What's wrong with it?' He held the ball out to her and laughing, Rachel backed away.

'Keep your prize.' She watched as he put it in his pocket, then sat closer to her. He obviously wasn't too distressed by his disagreement with Kylie. Rachel simply couldn't understand the pair. She hated to be at odds with anyone but Kylie and Prince acted as though it didn't mean anything.

Prince was studying her as though trying to ascertain her thoughts. 'So what's happening?'

Suddenly shy, Rachel shrugged. Maybe she should ask him to the mid-week Bible study. After all, his brother Blaze had started coming. But now he was looking directly at her with his dark magnetic eyes and perfect features and she found she simply couldn't do it. She couldn't think sensibly when he looked at her in that warm, direct way. The bell sounded, and relieved, she stood. 'Better get to class. Catch you later.'

She was aware of Prince's eyes following her and could have kicked herself. What was it she wanted from Prince? She wanted him to know and love God. That was it. She couldn't think any further because he wasn't a believer, he was probably a father, he was going out with her cousin – sort of – and he had a severe lack of morals. End of story.

Despite her efforts, Rachel couldn't stop thinking about Prince and the Bible study. She obviously couldn't ask him face to face. She'd tried that and failed. The written word was her best bet. She wrote a note, then went to put it in his locker. Prince never bothered to lock it. He told the other students he didn't have any possessions worth taking, anyway.

'Prince,' the note read in small, neat handwriting. 'My Dad is running a Bible study course for a few weeks to look at what Christians believe. I just wondered if you'd be interested. If you are, it's at my place every Wednesday at seven pm. I think Blaze is coming. Regards, Rachel.'

As she walked away from his locker, she grimaced, frustrated with herself. Why was it that she could be so expressive when it came to music and writing but face to face, she was hopeless?

She was walking to class with Jeff not more than half an hour later when Prince caught up with her.

'Hey, Rachel!'

She turned, looking embarrassed. 'Yeah?'

'I got your note, but sorry, I won't be able to come to your Bible study this week.'

Rachel nodded, not bothering to ask why. She didn't want Prince to feel pressured in any way. 'Okay.'

'You asked him?' Jeff demanded when Prince was out of earshot.

'Yeah.'

'Why?'

Rachel shrugged uncomfortably. 'I thought it would be good for him to learn about the faith.'

'You never asked him before he and Kylie broke up.'

So Jeff had heard about the fight between the two lovers. 'It's nothing to do with that.'

'What about Kylie? Why didn't you ask her?'

Rachel laughed. 'I have. Several times.'

'Well what about Brad Jenson?'

'Come on, Jeff, what is this really about?'

Jeff looked at her seriously, then sighed. 'I guess I'm jealous,' he admitted. 'I mean, Prince would never be accused of being a homosexual.'

'Maybe not, but he has poor moral standards. He already has a child, according to rumour. You, on the other hand, are good looking and have high standards, which in my opinion, makes you more of a man than Prince Clements will ever be.'

Jeff smiled, putting an arm around her. 'Thanks, Rachel. You always know what to say to make me feel better.'

His soft, deep voice in her ear warmed her heart and she smiled up at him, glad the tension in the air had lifted.

CHAPTER THIRTEEN

Rachel gazed at Prince, wishing her parents were not so far away. So many confusing emotions filled her and her father was not there to speak to about them. She loved Jeff. Yes, romantically. But what she felt for Prince was just as strong but so different. She was attracted to him, she had to admit that, but what girl wasn't? No, this feeling was something deeper that she couldn't put into words. A longing that everything would be right with him and God, that he could know the peace and joy that Rachel herself had found in knowing God.

Biting her lip, Rachel approached him. 'I just thought I'd ask you to our Bible study again. Dad's away but my grandfather is running it.'

'Yeah, I heard your Dad's away,' Prince nodded. 'Overseas or something.'

'He's in the Hanoa Strait Islands. His Dad's a missionary over there.'

'Missionary? As in working with cannibals and savages?'

Rachel laughed, knowing he was teasing. 'That's right. We don't know if he'll even return. I guess if he gets eaten I'll be looking after my baby brother.'

'You don't think they'll eat your brother too?'

'No, not enough meat on him.' Even as Rachel said it, her face showed her horror that she could even say such a thing. Her self-consciousness when looking Prince Clements in the face caused her to come out with ridiculous comments.

But Prince was laughing. 'Tell you what, I'll come to your meetings if your parents get savaged by those natives. Just to show you my support.'

Rachel laughed then, too. 'Deal.'

She saw Prince become tense. His gaze was now locked on Kylie, who was heading toward them.

'Don't bother with him, Rachel,' Kylie's pretty face sported an ugly sneer. 'He won't ever be religious. His standards are way below yours and everybody else's! He doesn't know anything about common decency or commitment.'

She flounced off and Prince flinched as students in the playground turned to watch his reaction. She touched his arm. 'Don't let Kylie get to you. She'll get over it.'

Prince frowned. 'I don't know about that. She's pretty upset with me. But it's okay. I can always go along to your Bible study thing if I get too lonely.'

Rachel chuckled. 'So you're saying it would take a disaster to get you there – either my parents have to be killed or you have to be permanently dumped by Kylie.'

He gave her a gentle punch on the shoulder. 'Funny, aren't you?'

She went to punch him back. 'I like to think so.'

He caught her hand with lightning reflexes and captured it in his. 'Enough of the violence. You need to learn to keep your hands to yourself.'

She pulled at her hand but he didn't let it go. His eyes twinkled. 'You don't mess with circus performers. We're fast and we're strong.'

Rachel felt familiar warmth begin to creep up her neck. 'I'm not the one who needs to keep my hands to myself right now.'

He looked down at her hand in his and gave his slow, amused smile. 'Good point.'

'So you going to let me go?'

He looked heavenward as though considering. His hand felt warm and strong around hers and Rachel wondered what would have happened if they hadn't been interrupted. Prince suddenly dropped her hand as though burned, his eyes now focused on something else.

Rachel looked up in surprise and concern. The school principal stood before her, holding out the phone. As she took it, he put an arm around her shoulder and ushered her to a quiet place a few metres away. He handed her the phone.

'Rachel, you need to take this.'

Confused, Rachel took the phone. What could be so urgent the school principal would bring her the phone in the middle of the playground? If something had happened to her parents, surely her grandparents would come and get her or the school would call her to the office and let her know?

'Hello?'

'Rachel.'

She sighed in relief at her father's voice. 'Dad, what's going on? Aren't you in the Hanoa Straits?'

'Yes. Rach, you remember our favourite Bible story?'

'Of course.'

'Sometimes the chariot that takes us up to heaven in a whirlwind is not pulled by horses. Sometimes God uses other means.'

She began to shake. 'Dad, what are you talking about? You're scaring me.'

'Don't be scared, Rach. God's timing is always perfect. Always.'

Fear made her angry. 'I know that. Just tell me, Dad. Has something happened to Mum?'

'Not yet.' She heard her father take in a deep breath and she made herself wait. Her heart hammered inside her chest and she knew that whatever he was about to say would be life-changing.

'We've been captured, Rach. We won't be coming home. But we love you and God loves you and he will be with you every step of the way.'

Captured? What was he talking about? 'But the government will help you. They help with things like this.'

His voice sounded sad. 'Not this time, Rachel. There's no time. Promise me one thing. Promise you'll follow God all the days of your life; that you will turn to him for comfort and trust him, even in this.'

A gunshot sounded and Rachel screamed. 'Dad? Dad!' Tears streamed down her face.

'It's okay, Rach. I'm still here.' He choked on his words. 'But Grandpa's not. He's safe in Jesus' arms.'

Rachel fought the hysteria rising in her throat. 'Let me talk to them, Dad. I'll stop them. I will! They'll listen to me!'

'Rach, it's time to say goodbye. I love you and Mum is right here beside me and she's saying she loves you, too. She's crying too much to speak, but always believe it, Rachel. We love you and we love Paul. Make sure he knows that when he is old enough to understand. And make sure he knows Jesus so we can see him again in heaven.'

'No, Dad, no!'

The phone went dead and Rachel sank to the ground. The principal tried to support her but ended up squatting down beside her, his hand gently resting on her shoulder.

'Rachel, I'm sorry. He said he didn't have long; said he *had* to speak to you.'

Rachel managed to calm herself enough to speak through her sobs. 'Mr Jenson, I think my parents are being executed. We have to do something!'

Mr Jenson's eyes widened. 'So I was right. I knew it was something serious and I asked my office ladies to call the police. They may have been able to track the call.'

He reached a hand to help her up. 'Come on, let's get you to the office and call your grandparents.' He looked out at the crowd of interested students. 'Shows over, boys and girls. Off you go.'

Rachel managed to look up. Prince stood a few metres away, comforting a distraught Kylie. She was encompassed in his arms and for the first time anger toward her cousin built up within her until she thought she would explode. Why couldn't Kylie see this wasn't about her? That it was she, Rachel who was most likely an orphan, she was the one who really needed the comfort. Only moments ago Kylie had been attacking Prince and it was she, Rachel, being a friend to him. And now it was she, Rachel, who desperately needed the comfort of a friend.

Rachel felt her eyes filling with tears again, but somewhere inside she felt numb. *I'm an orphan!* She wondered why such a thing would enter her mind at a time like this. She had always thought being an orphan was a romantic kind of an idea – a bit like Anne of Green Gables. Now she knew there was nothing romantic about it. It was a dark, cold, horrifying thing to be.

The wait in the office was excruciating. Mr Jenson tried to talk her through it and even brought in the school counsellor but in the end there was nothing to be done but wait. And pray. But she couldn't pray. It was as though a wall had come up between her and God and she couldn't get the words out.

Grandma and Grandpa Blythe arrived and sat with her until finally a police officer arrived at the school. His face was grim.

'I'm sorry. The news has come through and been confirmed that your parents and grandfather were shot and killed.'

Rachel stood. 'But why?' She had to try to make sense of what she was hearing. To make it real, if it really was.

'Rebel groups. They have been causing trouble for a while. Your parents were simply in the wrong place at the wrong time. They were taken as hostages. These groups know they will get more attention if they execute westerners.'

'And Paul? My little brother?'

'He's okay. He's in the hands of the authorities and will be brought back to Australia immediately.'

It was then that Rachel cried. Great, rasping sobs came from somewhere deep within as she tried to grasp the reality of what she was hearing. Surely there was some mistake? Through her mind flashed the vision of her parents as they had boarded the plane.

'I love you,' her father had assured her, 'and remember, we are sure to meet again.'

Rachel nodded, enjoying the words she had heard so often. It was the way her father had always said goodbye since she had given her life to God.

Then she stood before her mother, gazing down at little Paul. 'He's beautiful, isn't he?'

Her mother reached a hand and rested it on Rachel's cheek. 'And so are you.' She gazed into Rachel's eyes. 'You are beautiful inside and out. I'm proud of you, Rachel.'

Her mother had never said that before. Her father was the affectionate one, the one she was close to. Rachel had smiled absently but she treasured the words in her heart. Then she had said goodbye, never really believing it would be the last time.

As the memories flooded her mind, Rachel wondered why God had planned it this way. Why was she the one left behind?

'I don't want to be.' Anguish consumed her once more. 'Not as an orphan!'

Yet even in her overwhelming pain, a quiet, still voice calmed and reassured her soul. *You still have a Father. I am with you always.*

***

The funeral would not be for two weeks and Rachel couldn't bring herself to go to school. Neither could she bring herself to play the piano. Every time she saw it she remembered her father sitting beside her on the stool, singing along with her. She remembered her mother dusting and polishing that piano. Writing was now impossible. Her heart was too confused and full, yet at the same time, everything inside felt so empty and hollow. No words or music felt right. It was a mockery of the tragedy she was going through.

Her only comfort was the memory of her father's final words. He had not been afraid and he had known it was God's timing for him to go. She knew that as the trigger was pulled and the life-blood flowed from him he was being carried up in chariots of fire pulled by horses to his heavenly home. If only she could remember that when her heart jarred with the awful reality of the shooting.

It was a week before Paul returned home in the arms of a complete stranger. And on the same plane were the bodies of her mother and father. It seemed inappropriate, but feeling helpless, Rachel buried the ache and struggled on.

Paul smiled in delight as he reached his little arms out to Rachel. She rushed and took him, burying her face in his neck. He smelled like her parents. He had grown so much. She clung to him as he gave her slobbery baby kisses. She could tell he hadn't forgotten her and neither did he seem traumatised. But how could he be smiling? Didn't he miss their parents? Could he truly have no idea of the finality of the tragedy he had witnessed? He wrapped his chubby arms around her neck, gazing up at her with adoration and Rachel knew that to Paul, she was the only one who existed in that moment. Maybe that was the answer to her own survival. Live in each moment, forgetting the past and focusing only on what was in front of her. For the first time she believed she might survive.

Rachel was feeding Paul when a knock came at the door. She heard Grandpa Blythe go to answer it and her heart rate sped up. Visitors made her nervous. She never knew how she would react when they talked about her parents; whether she would laugh or cry. There was no predicting what her crazy emotions were going to do.

'Rachel, it's someone called Blaze Clements. Shall I invite him in?'

Rachel took a deep breath and nodded. When Blaze walked in she saw the compassion and sorrow in his eyes. He genuinely cared.

'Rachel, your father was like a father to me. My own father has never really taken on that role. He was a special man.'

Rachel could only nod and try to swallow around the lump in her throat.

Blaze shuffled, then sat down on the nearest chair. Grandpa sat, too.

'One day I showed your father our horses. He made a comment that they reminded him of the Bible story where Elijah was taken up into heaven in a chariot pulled by horses.' Blaze bit his lip, then let out a shaky sigh. 'I'd never read that story before, but he showed me where to find it in 2 Kings in the Bible. That night I read it and it's a pretty special story.'

Rachel felt the tears begin to flow unchecked down her face. There was no stopping them now. Blaze was looking at her earnestly.

'Rachel, if it's appropriate, I just wondered what you think about using two of our horses to pull the coffins to the church. Kind of as a send-off.' Blaze faltered as though he wasn't sure if his suggestion was crazy or unacceptable. 'I just thought it would be meaningful.'

Rachel nodded, trying to speak. He couldn't know just how meaningful and appropriate it would be, how much it would have meant to her father! Finally, all she could do was stand, throw her arms around Blaze and nod a yes. One day she would explain to Blaze but right now the words were stuck in her throat. He didn't seem to mind her inability to speak. He squeezed her in a brotherly hug then stepped back.

'I'll see what we can do about some kind of chariot.'

'I think I could work something out. You can leave that part to me.'

Blaze and Rachel turned to Grandpa at once. He rubbed his forehead. 'Well, it's just something I can do …'

Rachel managed to speak. 'Thank you, Grandpa.' Her eyes welled with tears once more. 'And thank you, Blaze.'

***

Rachel couldn't sleep. A rhythmic thump came from the workshed next door and she knew it wasn't Prince Clements bouncing balls down the roof this time. The sound of baby Paul's cry joined in. His distress tore at her already aching heart and threatened to suffocate her. She raced in to lift him from his cot, relieved when he snuggled into her neck and began to settle.

'It's all right, little brother. We're going to be all right.'

There was no choice, really. They had to be. The thump continued and Rachel moved to the window. Lights lit up the shed next door. Mr Tanner hadn't used that shed in years. What was he doing in there? She moved closer to the window, patting Paul gently on the back. Someone came out the shed. Grandma Blythe? It certainly looked like her but what was she doing in Mr Tanner's shed? The sound of an electric saw startled baby Paul and at the same time Grandma walked in the door. She stopped when she saw Rachel and Paul, then held out her arms.

'Let me take Paul. Why don't you go down and see what Grandpa is doing in your neighbour's shed?'

Rachel couldn't begin to imagine what Grandpa would be doing but she obediently slipped on a dressing gown and shoes and made her way across the garden. The light cast eerie shadows over the lawn and she breathed in a sob. Whose job would it be to mow the lawn now? Her eyes went to the washing line. Her mother would never stand there hanging out the clothes and enjoying the sunshine on a winter's morning ever again. But no, she couldn't allow herself to think that way. She had to survive for herself and for Paul. She had to remember her parents were in a place beyond all she could ever imagine, a place where there would be no more crying, no more pain. She would join them there someday. So why did she still feel so sad, so empty?

The light from the shed made her blink. She stood at the door, adjusting to the brightness. Then she saw it. Grandpa stood there with Mr Tanner and together they were building a chariot. It was wooden and simple but it was a chariot. Grandpa was sanding back the side and Rachel saw love in every swipe of the sandpaper against the grain of the wood. Grandpa had never been affectionate. He was very much like her mother, who spoke her love in actions and gifts. And here was his final act of love for his daughter.

He stopped when he saw Rachel and his wrinkled face softened. He reached out a well-worn hand and Rachel came.

'It's beautiful,' she whispered.

He smiled and a tear leaked from under his eyes. 'She doesn't need it, Rachel, but we do.'

She knew what he meant. The chariot would make no difference to her mother now but it would serve as a beautiful reminder that God had taken her up to heaven in his perfect timing.

Grandpa sat down on a solid metal toolbox and patted the place beside him. 'Sit with me a while?'

When she sat he wiped at the tear now down near his chin and rubbed his gnarled hands together. 'She always loved houses. She was so excited when she and your father finally had a house to call their own. She worked on it, painted it, cleaned it, made it home.'

Rachel smiled, remembering her mother up the ladder, painting her walls a beautiful lilac purple. 'She made it beautiful.'

Grandpa nodded. 'She just wanted to feel she fit in. We moved so much when she was a child and she just wanted a real, permanent home – somewhere to belong.' He swiped at another tear. 'And now she does, Rachel. Jesus said he was leaving earth to prepare a place for us so that we can be with him forever. She is where she belongs, in a place Jesus personally prepared for her.'

Grandpa shifted on the toolbox until he was looking directly in her eyes. 'But you know what's beautiful, Rach? I read those verses in Matthew 14 again last night, and Jesus also says he will come back to get us to take us to be with him. Your mother wasn't alone at any point. There's no point between life and death that we cross alone. He is there every step of the way.'

Rachel felt her lip quivering and bit it. A peace began to steal over her. She had dreaded the thought of her parents being afraid and alone in their final minutes but they weren't. Just as she wasn't. The same Jesus who loved and never left her parents also loved and would never leave her.

'We're going to survive this, aren't we, Grandpa?'

Grandpa nodded and reached a tentative hand to her cheek. 'Yes, Rachel. We will have our moments of overwhelming grief and that is normal. But in God's strength, we will get through this.'

***

When Blaze Clements saw the chariot he asked permission to paint flames down the side. Grandpa agreed and Rachel sat on the metal toolbox, watching him paint. Blaze was clearly a gifted artist.

'Starre and Beauty own our white horses,' he told her as he worked. 'They were keen for us to use them. It's so good to just be able to do something to help.'

'They were?' Rachel was surprised. Starre and Beauty were the more reserved and less well-liked of the Clements family.

Blaze nodded. 'We felt so helpless when Bonnie got burned. There was nothing we could do. But this is something we can do.'

He hesitated and dipped his brush slowly back into the orange paint. Rachel looked at the orange flames streaking the side of the chariot and suddenly felt for Blaze. How must it feel to be painting flames after that awful experience when Bonnie was burned? And with a name like Blaze, there was never any way he could really escape the memory of the fire.

'It must have been hard, the fire.'

He glanced at her before painting again. 'It was. It still is.' He swallowed hard. 'In a way it was like the old Bonnie died.' Realising what he had said, his dark eyes widened. 'Sorry. That's so insensitive of me.'

Rachel shook her head. 'No, it's okay. I heard Bonnie left town.'

87

Blaze nodded. 'Yes. But I'll never give up praying for her.' He put down the brush and looked at her, his eyes sparkling in the light. 'I know it's wrong to feel so attracted to someone who doesn't share my faith. It just won't work. But even though I've prayed about it, I can't get rid of these feelings I have for her.' He looked down. 'Is that terrible?'

Was it terrible? If she said it was, she would be condemning herself, because if she was honest, she was attracted to Prince Clements and that feeling just wouldn't go away.

Before she could answer, footsteps sounded down the path. Rachel glanced at Blaze and an unspoken message passed between them. Their conversation would go on hold for now.

'Prince. What are you doing here?'

Prince leaned against the wall of the shed and gave his slow smile. 'Thought I'd see how it's coming along.' He looked at Rachel and his expression became serious. 'And how you are coming along?'

Rachel shrugged as tears filled her eyes. The mere suggestion of compassion or understanding from anyone seemed to set her off. Why couldn't she control these emotions?

Prince came and sat beside her and his arm came around her. 'Where's your boyfriend when you need him?'

Rachel shrugged. Jeff was out performing somewhere again but she couldn't speak right now.

Prince pulled her closer and she leaned into him, feeling the firm security of his strong chest and feeling protected and loved. Then her eyes caught Blaze's and she pulled back as understanding passed through his expression. He knew.

'Pray for me.' She mouthed the words and Blaze nodded. He came and reached a hand to Rachel to pull her up and away from Prince. He flourished the paint brush toward the chariot.

'So what do you think?'

Rachel knew she had been rescued and smiled. 'Thank you.' Her words were laced with meaning.

'You're welcome.'

The understanding between her and Blaze was a timely reminder that she and Prince could never have that spiritual connection. Without that, it simply couldn't work.

Prince stood and stretched. 'Well, looks like you two are doing just fine in here.' He headed toward the door, then looked back over his shoulder. 'Should I let your boyfriend know?'

Rachel's brows rose. What did he mean by that? 'Know what?'

Prince kept walking. 'That he should be here supporting you.'

Rachel bit her lip and Blaze gave her a lopsided smile. 'Pray for me too?'

She nodded.

***

Rachel and her grandparents spent the next week making funeral plans and caring for baby Paul. The day of the funeral dawned a clear and glorious day. The chariot sat out the front of the house, waiting for Blaze to bring the two white circus horses to collect it. From there they would pick up the coffins from the undertaker and go to the church.

The town came out in force for the funeral. Many spoke words of comfort and reassurance to Rachel, telling her how touched they had been by her parents' lives over the years, and how much they were respected.

Rachel clung to little Paul and lifted her chin as she looked around at the crowds of people her parents had loved and cared for. Their death was not going to be in vain, she decided. They had taught her about God, shown her his love and lived a life of faith before her. Determination filled her as she pictured her Mum and Dad. *I will follow their example. I will share my faith with others. I won't be ashamed or afraid. I will be bold and courageous. And I will make sure Paul grows to know and love God. I will teach him everything Mum and Dad were going to teach him.*

She allowed her grandmother to take Paul from her arms but she suddenly felt bereft. Life would be empty if it weren't for Paul. God had been so merciful in sending her a brother but she was also afraid of losing the only family she had left.

Crossing her empty arms across her chest, Rachel glanced around to see Blaze Clements standing silently by the graveside, his pimpled face showing he shared her anguish as tears dripped down his cheeks and off his chin. He caught her eye and came over, putting a brotherly arm around her shoulder. 'I really am so sorry, Rachel.'

He passed her his hanky as her tears flowed once more. She had her own pocket full of tissues but his gesture was so touching she found comfort in receiving it.

'We know where they are.' His dark eyes were intense, imploring her to believe.

'We do,' she agreed, 'and I'm happy for them, but sad for Paul and I. Especially Paul.'

'Because he won't remember them?'

'And because he won't have their example to follow. But Blaze, I'm going to do everything in my power to be that example for him, to make sure he knows Christ.'

Blaze gazed at her thoughtfully for a moment, then nodded. 'It puts it all in perspective, doesn't it? Knowing God – being prepared for death is what really matters.'

'And sharing it with others while you can,' Rachel added, then broke down again. 'Sorry,' she said brokenly through tears. 'I just so badly want this all to bring good. I know God can bring good from anything … but this?'

Blaze's arm tightened around her. 'Rachel, believe me, it already has done good. God has used your parents' lives to teach me how to follow Christ. And their death has challenged me to take every opportunity to share my faith. More than ever, I want to be a minister!'

Her eyes widened. 'You do?'

'Yes, and as we just talked about your little brother something really hit me. I have got to make some major changes in my life.'

'Changes?' Rachel yearned for anything that might show her God's reason for taking her beloved parents.

'Well, I believe God wants me to gain guardianship of Sky, Prince's baby girl, and teach her the ways of God. She's in a foster home right now but I can't leave her there.'

Rachel's eyes filled with hope but she was jarred as another arm came around her shoulder and moved her away from Blaze's comforting words and touch. It was Jeff.

'How are you going?'

She looked at him and felt nothing. There was something shallow about those good looks and amazingly deep voice. What could she say?

He patted her shoulder. 'Don't overdo it, will you? You're living on adrenaline right now but it will soon run out.'

'I'm okay.'

He glanced at Blaze. 'I'll just steal her away for a bit if you don't mind.'

As he led her to a seat nearby, Rachel wished she had the nerve to tell him that she minded even if Blaze didn't. She had seen very little of Jeff when she first heard the news of her parents' deaths. She understood that he would feel awkward and not know how to comfort her, but Blaze and Prince would have felt the same way. Yet they made an effort to be there for her and understand. She glanced apologetically in Blaze's direction. Blaze gave her a knowing smile. He understood and wasn't offended.

As mourners left the cemetery, Rachel took her baby brother in her arms again and stood by the wooden coffins deep in the ground. The flowers covering them seemed such a meagre gift to offer the two people who had meant so much to her.

'I'm going to offer you greater respects than that,' she whispered. 'I'm going to follow your example and live every moment for God.'

She stopped as little Paul reached for her face with a delighted smile and gurgle of appreciation.

'I'm going to teach you all about them, Paul.' She couldn't help smiling back at him. 'They're not here. They're in heaven with God but we can meet them there one day.'

Even as she spoke them, the words began to sink in. *They're home! And not a moment before God intended them to be. They lived every moment he planned for them and they lived it to his glory.*

She stopped Paul's hand as he reached his fist to grip her hair in his slobbery fingers. 'I'm going to show you the way to heaven, little brother. But whether or not you get there is up to you. I pray with all my heart you will go the right way!'

The awesome responsibility that was on her weighed her down for a few moments before she smiled and looked to heaven. 'I'm not alone. God will give me strength every step of the way.'

CHAPTER FOURTEEN

Rachel heard her grandmother's shuffling footsteps as she went to answer the door. Grandma and Grandpa Blythe had decided to move in until Rachel finished her schooling and Rachel was relieved. She needed some stability and her grandparents provided that.

'Rachel, it's Kylie,' Grandma called. Rachel looked up from where she was sitting with baby Paul in her arms.

'Hey, Rach,' Kylie acknowledged. Her tone was hesitant, her expression subdued.

Rachel smiled, glad to see her cousin, then smiled wider as Paul struggled to sit up and gave a happy giggle as he looked at her.

'He's a social bug,' Kylie said, allowing the baby to grasp her finger.

'He is,' Rachel agreed. 'Unlike me.'

'Yeah, but you're a mother now.'

Rachel could tell Kylie was not impressed with the idea, but nothing would stop her from caring for her little brother. True, her grandparents were his guardians until Rachel was eighteen, but she already felt a fierce protectiveness for him.

'So when are you coming back to school?' Kylie asked. 'I haven't seen you for ages.'

'I thought I'd come back tomorrow. Not that I'll be able to concentrate properly.'

Kylie looked at her with sympathy. 'So long as you do your

best. That's what matters. I know they'll make allowances for what you've been through with your parents and everything.'

Rachel noticed once again that Kylie avoided using the word 'death'. She had walked around the topic for weeks now. Gathering up courage, she looked into the eyes of the cousin she had once been so close to.

'Kylie, I know where they are. I'm sad that they died, but I'm okay. I know I'll meet them again in heaven someday.'

To Rachel's surprise, Kylie jumped up angrily from the chair. 'I'm sick of hearing that, Rachel Seton! All this lovely romantic stuff about them being in heaven so it's okay that it happened. Well it's not okay! We're never going to see them again. They were shot! Murdered by rebels. My aunty and uncle were murdered and I'm the only one who cares. It's like you all think it's unspiritual to grieve!'

'It's not that,' Rachel began, but Kylie was shaking her head.

'You haven't written a song since it happened, have you?' she asked accusingly. 'Have you?'

'No.'

'Well do it, Rachel. Face up to reality. Heaven or no heaven, we won't be seeing them for years. Let it sink in and stop acting like I'm the one with problems.'

Rachel stared at Kylie, not knowing what to say. She was sad and missed her parents horribly. Kylie couldn't know just how many tears she'd cried. But she longed for Kylie to see death the way she could. Not an ending without hope, but rather the beginning of a new life in heaven.

When Kylie left, Rachel went into her room and took up a pen. Slowly, painfully, she began to write.

'I will not think of death as meaning life is through.
The final gasp of breath was not the end of you.
And yet I weep to think I'm now here all alone,

until that day when I will join you in our home.

As Rachel wrote, she became more determined to live her life for God. It was so short. She didn't know when her last moment might come. She must share her faith with Kylie and with Prince. She couldn't let Kylie see just how confused and hurt she really was or Kylie might think she had lost her faith and faith was all she had right now.

'*I will always love you.*' God's quiet voice in her heart gave her comfort and yet still she tightly controlled all she felt inside. She was too afraid to set it free.

***

It was hard to return to school but most students were nicer to her than they had ever been. Kylie seemed sorry for her outburst of the day before and sat with Rachel in any classes Jeff didn't share. Jeff was trying harder to be a support, not often speaking, but always being ready with a comforting hand on her shoulder or an understanding look.

Although Prince didn't mention her loss, he seemed to make it his ambition to take the sad look from her face and make her smile.

'Where's my pen?' Rachel glanced around her desk as the Maths class began. It had been there just moments before.

'Prince has it.' Kylie chuckled, a sparkle in her eyes. Rachel glanced at Prince, who was bent over his work book. However, there was no pen in his hand or on his desk.

'Prince, have you seen,' she began, then burst into laughter as he looked up. His cheeks were filled out in the shape of a pen. 'What on earth are you doing?'

He grinned, his mouth looked as though it was stretched to breaking point. He reached in and took the pen out, holding it out to her. Rachel moved backward as he came toward her with it.

'What's up? Scared of boy germs?'

'No, just of saliva.'

'But saliva has healing properties.' His dark eyes sparkled with mischief.

'Maybe, but I prefer my own.'

Prince shrugged, wiped the pen down his shirt and put it in his pocket before returning to his work.

'You can fit anything in that mouth of yours!' Rachel muttered, remembering the tennis ball that had been in there a few months ago. She began searching in her pencil case for another pen but someone else had stepped out of their seat and was holding one out to her. It was Brad.

'Here. I've got a spare one.'

Rachel eyed him suspiciously and he gave a lopsided smile. 'I haven't sucked it, I promise. I'm trying to be nice.'

He looked awkward and Rachel grinned despite her amazement. 'Wow, Brad Jenson, I can't believe it.'

He frowned. 'Why? I'm allowed to be nice sometimes. It's not like I've said I'll become a God-boy or anything.'

She met his eyes. 'Not yet, anyway. But I'm praying for you.'

This time it was Brad's turned to look flabbergasted as Rachel reached to take the pen. Why didn't she fear his teasing anymore? What had changed? Even she didn't know for sure, but she took the pen from his hand.

'Thanks. I appreciate it.' She shook her head as she turned back to work. She really did appreciate the way people were trying to make her feel better, but it also served as a continual reminder of her grief. If only everything would go back to normal she might be able to forget. But how could such a thing be forgotten? No, instead she would just need to make sure it wasn't in vain. The best thing she could think to do was tell as many people about God as she could.

She saw Prince taking a text book from his locker after class and approached him with a new confidence and purpose. 'Do you want to come to Bible study tonight?'

'Tonight? I'll give it a miss.'

'Remember our deal.' She gave a rueful laugh. 'You said you'd come to Bible study if my parents didn't come back.'

'No, the deal was I would come if they were eaten by cannibals.' A smile tugged at his lips.

'That's true.' Rachel became tentative. 'Do I annoy you, asking you to things all the time?'

He gave her his engaging smile. 'Nah, keep asking. You never know, I might come eventually.' He looked beyond her and Rachel followed his gaze. Jeff was there waiting for her. He raised his brow and Rachel knew he was impatient. She rushed to his side, throwing her back pack on her shoulder.

'Sorry. Let's go.'

He gave her an intense look as they walked out the school gate. 'You don't spend much time in the music room anymore.'

She gave him a cheeky look. 'I don't have a chance. You're in there all the time.'

He didn't share her smile. 'You haven't written a song since your parents died.'

Rachel nodded seriously, her voice softening. 'I can't. The music has gone from me. I have no heart to sing. My life is not a melody anymore.'

'Then what is it?'

She shrugged. 'Nothing. There's just no music there.'

He put an arm around her. 'Don't worry. It will come back. There will be music in your life again one day.'

As Rachel looked up at him, she longed with all her heart to believe his words. But she had a feeling it would be a long time before she could sit down at a piano again without grief threatening to smother her every thought and emotion.

CHAPTER FIFTEEN

The end of the school year came and Rachel was relieved. She needed time to sort out her heart and emotions. She heard that Blaze Clements had been accepted into Bible college and there was a sweet sadness in the news. He said he wanted to be like her father and though that was a compliment, she didn't want to feel that God was training someone else up to replace him.

There wasn't a day that went by when Rachel's thoughts didn't return to her parents and all they had taught her. In spending time with God, she felt she had a connection with them, for after all, they were in heaven with him. Often she would find herself asking God to tell them things.

'Do you think it's wrong to still try to tell them things?' she asked Jeff one evening as they sat on her verandah, looking out into the night.

Jeff looked at her seriously. 'I don't think so. That night I first became a Christian your Dad told me about a verse in the Bible that talks about there being a great cloud of witnesses watching over us.'

'Witnesses?'

'Yeah. Like other believers who have already died. People like Abraham and Moses. Maybe that includes your parents.'

Rachel looked up into the night sky, gazing at the clouds that had gathered. Her parents were truly there! She smiled a little, hoping they knew she was okay and that she was more bold and determined to tell people about God.

'I think the verse is in Romans or something like that,' Jeff was saying. 'The apostle Paul said it. He talks about the cloud of witnesses cheering us on.'

Rachel smiled, knowing she would look it up as soon as she had some time alone. The thought appealed to her.

'You're so different from when I first met you.' Jeff put an arm around her and drew her closer.

'I am? How?'

He shrugged. 'I don't know. Maybe you're more confident.'

'In a good way?'

He laughed, coming even closer. 'Yes, in a good way.' His eyes locked with hers and for a moment she hoped he would kiss her. But he averted his eyes and pulled back. Rachel couldn't help the disappointment that filled her. Her own parents had such a loving, affectionate relationship and she found herself longing for the same thing now that they were gone.

Jeff seemed willing enough to touch her at school but whenever they were alone, he became distinctly uncomfortable. He would often put an arm around her shoulder or hold her hand but it was big-brotherly. Rachel tried not to let it bother her but found herself often wondering about it.

***

Christmas was different that year. Baby Paul loved it, playing happily in the wrapping paper and making Rachel laugh more than she had for a long time. Every day she thanked God for her brother, knowing that without him she would have felt lost and alone.

Jeff got himself a holiday job in one of the clubs and she saw little of him but didn't mind. Grandpa taught her to drive and her days were busy and full. It was when she lay alone at night that deep sadness would engulf her and tears would flow in earnest. She missed her parents every moment of every day. Sometimes they seemed so close she could hear their voices and at other times she couldn't even remember what they looked like. It was at those times she would panic and scrabble around for a photo to feast her eyes on their beloved faces.

It was Rachel who mowed the lawn. Grandpa was getting older and it wore him out. Grandma insisted on doing all the washing despite her arthritis and Rachel knew it was her way of showing her love. Kylie stayed away, spending a lot of time with Prince, and Rachel didn't blame her. Kylie had never liked work and she had never particularly liked Grandma and Grandpa, either.

'They're too set in their ways,' she told Rachel. 'They've forgotten what it means to be young and have fun.'

Rachel knew it was more than that. Grandma and Grandpa were never afraid to tell Kylie she needed God. She was relieved when Kylie went up North with her family for a few weeks, giving her even more space.

So it surprised her when Prince and his triplets turned up on her doorstep a few days later.

'We thought you might be looking for something to do,' Prince said with a warm smile. 'And we wondered if you're interested in riding.'

Rachel's eyes widened as she shifted Paul in her arms. He was reaching for the elegant Misty, who dimpled at him then looked to Rachel, her eyes questioning. Rachel smiled and handed Paul over. He wrapped his arms around Misty's neck and then made a grab for her hair. Starre seemed just as taken with him and chatted away, responding to his baby gurgles.

'So, you interested?' Prince asked, not even seeming to notice baby Paul and his sisters.

Rachel's heart beat harder at the way he looked at her. 'I'd love to, but I've never been on a horse before.'

'Never?' Misty was gently disentangling her hair from Paul's fingers as she glanced at Rachel in disbelief.

'No, but only because I've never had the opportunity.'

Prince waved his arm toward the horses standing near the front of the house. 'Well, this is your opportunity. We brought a horse for you, but maybe you should ride with one of us until you learn how.'

Rachel felt her heart quicken with excitement. She hadn't been out for a long time and she never dreamed she would have the opportunity to ride the Clements family horses.

'I'll just check with my grandparents.'

Grandma looked hesitant when Rachel asked, but then smiled. 'Yes, go Rachel. You deserve a break.' She took Paul from Misty's arms and stood at the door, looking at the horses waiting patiently by the front gate.

Prince must have noticed Grandma's apprehension. 'Don't worry, they're well trained. And we won't let her fall off.'

Grandma nodded and gave a rather forced smile. 'I trust you. I guess I just have trouble letting my loved ones go.'

Rachel suddenly felt a lump in her throat and swallowed hard. If Grandma weren't such a reserved person she would have thrown her arms around her neck and hugged her. Instead, she just smiled at her in understanding. 'Thanks for letting me go, Grandma. I promise I'll be careful.'

Grandma gave a dismissive nod and headed back inside. Rachel wondered if she was leaving before she changed her mind. Her eyes followed her grandmother and Paul into the house before turning back to Prince and his sisters. They were looking at her with unveiled enthusiasm.

Prince leapt onto his horse. 'So you coming up with me?'

Rachel looked up at him and swallowed hard. Sitting up there with him would be dangerous for her heart and emotions. Her eyes darted to Misty's and Misty smiled.

'No, Prince. She's riding with me.'

Rachel shot her a silent thank you with her eyes and came to stand beside her. To her relief, Starre came to her side as well. 'I'll help you up.'

***

Horse riding was nothing like Rachel had imagined. It didn't take long to get over her fear of being up so high on a moving creature, especially with Misty behind her, helping hold her steady.

The triplets were good teachers and she was soon cantering on her own on a small horse called Penny Drop.

'Did you hear Blaze has gone to Bible college?' Prince asked when they all sat beneath a tree for a break.

'Already?'

Misty nodded. 'They don't start till next week, but Blaze was keen to get to the city and settle in. He's pretty excited.'

Rachel smiled, the usual bittersweet feeling overcoming her. 'I hope he enjoys it.'

Prince laughed, picking at the stick he had been stripping the bark off. 'Oh, he will. And we will, too. No more preaching for a while.'

'Prince!' Starre tried to quieten her brother, nodding toward Rachel.

Prince merely grinned as he glanced at Rachel, then back to Starre. 'It's okay. She knows where I stand with God.'

Rachel made herself look at him. 'Do I? Where do you stand, Prince?'

Prince shrugged, then chuckled. 'Actually, I don't know.'

Starre rolled her eyes. 'So how is Rachel s'posed to know where you stand?'

Prince threw down the stick he had been holding and stood. 'She's pretty perceptive. She'll work it out.' He looked at her directly and she drew in a breath. Why did he look at her that way? With that smoldering, almost tender look with some kind of underlying meaning? Did he enjoy doing that to all girls? Or was he not even aware he was doing it?

He held out a hand to help her up but she stood on her own. He then reached to help his sisters up and they accepted as though they were used to him doing it. Maybe he was just naturally charming and thoughtful. He turned to catch her studying him and smiled.

'You worked it out yet?'

Worked him out or worked out where he stood with God? She shook her head. 'No.'

He came up close, leading Penny Drop. 'Well, looks like I might just have to come to your Bible study meetings. Then we can both work it out.'

Rachel took Penny Drop from him with a smile. She doubted he would ever come to a meeting but she could always hope and pray. For now she would enjoy spending time with him and his sisters. She hadn't missed her parents or even thought of them the whole day.

***

She was surprised to find Jeff waiting when she arrived home. He was settled in the lounge room, playing with Paul.

'I hear you've been out on the town.' He kept his eyes on Paul.

'Not exactly on the town. I went riding with the triplets.'

'I know. They were talking about it at work.'

Rachel frowned in confusion and he met her eyes with a level look. 'Seems the Clements family feel a bit sorry for you.'

'What do you mean?'

He moved over on the lounge and patted the space beside him with one hand while still balancing Paul on his knee with the other. Rachel came and sat down, still cautious.

'What do you mean?' she asked again.

'Just that they all decided I wasn't spending enough time with you and that you needed a distraction.' His eyes met hers. 'Do you feel like I'm neglecting you? Is that why you went?'

Rachel's brows rose in surprise. 'Neglecting me? No, I just went because I thought it would be fun. I don't expect you to entertain me. You've got work and I'm a big girl.'

103

He took her hand and smiled. 'Well, next time you need to get out, I want you to give me a call, okay? I'll come and get you and take you somewhere a bit less risky. Somewhere that won't leave your Grandma scared of losing you.'

So Grandma had told him her concerns. Had it been selfish of her to go despite her grandmother's fears? And what about Jeff's job? She couldn't get him to have a day off just because she'd like to get out.

'Promise me?' His eyes bored into hers.

'I promise.'

Her heart sank because she knew that next time the triplets turned up at her door she would long to go with them but she would have to say no. She was confined to the house.

***

When the new school year arrived, Rachel didn't feel ready. She looked at herself in the mirror and shook her head. Not only did her brown eyes look tired and sad, she had put on weight and her uniform didn't sit quite right. Hanging around the house looking after Paul hadn't helped. There was comfort in food and Grandma was good at baking cakes and biscuits.

'Hey, Rachel!'

Rachel turned to see Kylie in her doorway. Grandma must have let her in. Kylie's eyes widened as she studied her.

'You've put on weight.'

Rachel felt tears sting her eyes. She held them in. 'I know.'

Kylie shrugged. 'Oh well, it kind of suits you. I thought I'd walk to school with you. Our final year. Can you believe it?'

Rachel forced a smile and picked up her school bag. There were lots of things she still couldn't believe. Like that she was an orphan whose parents were killed by rebels on a foreign island.

'I can't wait to see Prince. He spent most of his holidays riding that smelly horse of his. He asked me to come too but there was no way I was going near it.'

Rachel chuckled. 'I hope you don't call it a smelly horse in front of him.'

'No, I'm not that silly. And his little sister would scratch my eyes out if I did.'

Rachel had to agree. She wouldn't dare risk angering Beauty Clements, either.

A thundering of hooves could be heard as they neared the school and Kylie pointed. 'Look, here they come.'

Dust flew in the air as the family rode into the paddock beside the school. As always, Rachel's eyes were drawn to Prince. It had been hard to turn down his offers to ride during the holidays. After she refused the second offer he hadn't come again. She watched as he leaped from the horse and ran his hand through his wavy dark hair. It felt as though she were watching a movie and Prince was the hero. She shook herself. True, Jeff had hardly spent any time with her in the holidays but he was her boyfriend and thinking about Prince so much was not helpful.

Kylie rushed toward Prince, and Rachel made herself look away and walk in the gate. Time to go and find Jeff.

***

The school day seemed long and Rachel avoided Prince as best she could. She was walking out the gate when, instead of going to his horse, he called to her. She stopped and waited until he reached her, glad Jeff didn't seem to be around.

'I finally came to your Bible meetings in the holidays, since you wouldn't come riding with me.'

'Yeah, right.' She grinned, but he shook his head and his eyes were serious.

'I did. There was no one there so I went home again.'

Rachel stared, longing to see an expression that would show he was joking but there was none. 'You came in the holidays?'

'Yes. Last week.'

Rachel swallowed hard. 'It's not on in the holidays.' Her voice came out hoarse as she realised what had happened. 'I'm so sorry. I never thought to tell you that.'

Prince shrugged. 'It's okay.' He looked distractedly toward the gate where his brothers and sisters were waiting for him.

Rachel couldn't just leave it at that. 'What about next week?' She began scrabbling in her bag. 'There's a new day and time. I'll write it down for you.'

'Maybe later.' He gave her a dismissive wave and headed back to his horse. He effortlessly leaped onto its back and in a moment he was gone. Rachel stared after him. If only she'd believed him when he said he might come to a Bible study. She could have made sure he knew when and where it was. Now she had missed her chance.

'Fight, fight, fight!'

She turned to see what was happening and her heart constricted.

'It's Brad Jenson and Storm Clements,' she heard a voice say at her side.

'Storm? He's only little –' Rachel turned to Kylie, but Kylie was already on her way to watch the action. Rachel shook her head. She didn't understand why so many students took such pleasure in these awful events.

Rachel found herself drawn along in the crowd until she stood amongst the students. Peering over their shoulders, she saw Brad sneering at young Storm Clements, who was obviously furious. His hair was in a mess and it looked like he was going to fly at Brad at any moment.

'What happened?' Rachel asked the student beside her.

'Brad threw a rock at Dusty Lane.'

'Dusty Lane?'

'Storm's horse.'

Then Rachel understood why the small Storm Clements would fight someone so much bigger and older than he was.

Those horses were like humans to the circus family.

'Come on, hit me,' Brad taunted, reaching out and ruffling Storm's mass of curly hair. 'Or isn't your shabby ol' horse worth it?'

Rachel felt anger rising up within her at Brad's immature provocation and watched as Storm flew at Brad. Brad simply caught the boy's fist and twisted his arm around behind his back.

'Punch me now, circus clown.' Brad was caught off guard as Storm did a back flip and kicked out hard. His foot landed in Brad's stomach and knocked him backwards for a moment. The crowd cheered while Storm stepped back, ready for more.

'Okay, smarty.' Brad was clearly angry that the crowd was on Storm's side. 'Let's see you show off now.'

With that, he grabbed Storm around the waist and threw him to the ground. Rachel winced as she heard Storm moan. Then she watched in horror as Brad stood back and prepared to kick the boy. In a flash, a vision of young Paul went through her mind, and with reflexes like lightning, she shoved her way through the crowd and stood before Brad.

'Don't you dare!' she screamed at him. 'What do you think you're doing, picking on someone so much smaller than you?'

Brad seemed amused for a moment, then pushed her out of the way.

'Move it, religious girl.' He headed back toward Storm who was back on his feet. In an instant, Rachel was there again and Brad's raised fist came at her hard.

She had never felt such pain before, as fire hit her face. She fell to the ground with the force of the blow. For a moment, things went black and her ears rang. Then students were swarming around her, asking if she was all right and telling Brad off for hitting a girl.

'I didn't mean to.' Brad's voice came out horrified as he attempted to defend himself. 'She got in the way.'

Then Jeff was there, helping her sit up, his strong arms supporting her.

'What happened?' He gently wiped the blood from Rachel's nose with his shirt sleeve. 'Who did this?'

'Brad punched her,' a student called and Jeff looked as though he would explode. He looked around then jumped up. 'Where is he?'

To Rachel's relief, the principal himself appeared.

'Brad, Storm – get to my office!' He rushed to Rachel's side. The moment he saw her condition he turned to Kylie.

'Kylie, go to the office and ask Mrs Stark to call an ambulance.'

Rachel saw the blurry image of Kylie rushing to the office. The principal turned to Jeff. 'Can you lift her?'

Jeff nodded and Rachel felt him put his muscled arms beneath her, then lift her from the ground. She gasped as dizziness passed over her, then she focused on Jeff. His eyes were full of concern as he looked down at her and he seemed to carry her effortlessly toward the office.

He gave a grin. 'I've wanted to hold you this close for a long time. Didn't think it would take something like this for me to have my chance, though.'

Rachel let out a small laugh, then groaned in pain.

'Don't laugh,' Jeff told her and Rachel felt something inside melt at his caring words and his touch. Maybe it was worth this awful pain she was suffering.

As Rachel and Jeff waited for the ambulance, Prince came rushing into the room.

'Is Storm okay?' He stopped short as he saw Rachel.

'Yes, he's okay,' Jeff told him coolly, 'Thanks to Rachel. As you can see, she stepped in the way of the punch your brother deserved.'

'What on earth made you do something like that?' Prince's eyes were wide and Rachel wondered if he was more shocked by her appearance or what she had done. She raised red, swollen eyes to his and swallowed hard. 'I have a little brother, Prince, and there's no way I'd let Brad Jenson even touch him!'

'But Storm's not your brother.'

'No, but he's someone's little brother. Brad has no right to pick on someone so much smaller than he is.'

Prince said nothing as he studied her. Finally, he spoke. 'Thank you for what you did.' He gave a wry smile. 'Though I don't think Storm will be real happy that a girl came to his rescue.'

'At least I saved him from being beaten up.' Rachel dabbed at the blood streaming from her nose.

'Yeah,' Prince agreed, then began to laugh.

'What's so funny?'

'You.'

'Me?'

'Yeah. I used to think you were quiet. When I first met you you seemed so shy, you never pushed yourself forward, and now, suddenly, bang! You're right out there in the middle of a fight with Brad Jenson.'

'Stop making her talk!' Jeff ordered Prince angrily. 'Can't you see she's in no condition for a conversation?'

Prince shrugged. 'I think she can judge that for herself.'

Jeff glared harder. 'No, she can't. She's too polite and self-sacrificial to admit it kills her every time she even smiles.'

Prince glanced from Jeff's angry face to Rachel. For the first time, Rachel saw Prince angry. His dark eyes became darker, his expression like thunder. 'Your boyfriends a jerk,' he said over his shoulder, before stalking from the room without another word.

Jeff watched him go, then looked sincerely at Rachel. 'Sorry,' he said. 'I just hate seeing you in pain.'

Rachel nodded, unable to help forgiving him when he looked at her that way.

CHAPTER SIXTEEN

Rachel returned to school two days later, wishing she could wear sunglasses to hide her black eyes. Prince was the first to see her as she came in the school gate and his mouth tilted into a smothered grin. 'So I hear Brad broke it.'

Rachel reached a hand self-consciously to her swollen nose and nodded.

'It suits you.'

'What does?'

'That blue and black eye-shadow you've put around your eyes.'

Rachel laughed, knowing she looked a sight. 'Yes, it took me quite a while to get them looking so terrible.' She stopped as Jeff headed their way.

Prince followed her gaze. 'I'd better be going or I might get some black eyes too.' He walked away without even looking at Jeff. Jeff didn't seem to notice. When he reached Rachel, he ran a finger down her swollen face.

'How's it going?'

She shrugged. 'Good, but I'm a bit embarrassed about my black eyes. Everyone keeps staring.'

Jeff grinned. 'Do *I*?'

Rachel smiled back. 'I don't mind if *you* do. It's just everyone else.'

Jeff nodded, taking her hand in his. 'Remember, it's what God thinks that matters, not everyone else.'

Rachel laughed. It was only days ago she had told Jeff she was finally learning not to care what people thought of her.

'Don't preach my sermons back at me!' she chided with teasing in her tone. 'Or I might just stop preaching them at all.'

Immediately, Jeff pretended to look horrified. 'No, Rachel, please don't stop preaching!'

Rachel couldn't help laughing as she playfully slapped him. People were staring even more, but now she didn't care. She found herself growing more fond of Jeff as he made more effort to be a support. Her only regret was the way he was so protective of her. At first her relationship with him had created an easy, familiar friendship with all other males in her class, but now Jeff was making sure he was her only friend. Rachel could never seem to find any time to talk with Prince. Whenever he was nearby, Jeff would be there, demanding her full attention.

Today, Rachel knew she needed to reach Prince some other way. The only way seemed to be through letters. So at lunch time she crept away from Jeff, wrote Prince a note and slid it into his locker. To her dismay, Jeff arrived just as she closed the locker. His eyebrows rose in suspicion.

'What were you doing?'

Rachel flushed guiltily although she had done nothing wrong. 'Just putting a reminder about Bible study in his locker.'

'Why?'

Rachel frowned. If only Jeff would see past his own fears and allow her to reach out to others. 'Because he came to the wrong address last time. And it would be good if he came and heard about Jesus.'

Jeff cupped her chin in his hand and made her look at him. 'Rachel, if he comes it will only be because *you* asked him, not because he wants to hear about Jesus.'

Rachel said nothing. She didn't mind why people came so long as they came!

Jeff shook his head as he released her chin and stepped back, raking a hand through his hair in frustration. 'You have no idea, do you Rachel?'

'Of what?'

'The way guys think. Prince will see this as a come on. You know what type of guy he is.'

Rachel laughed, but Jeff was clearly angry. 'Okay, go chase the charmer.' He turned away, but Rachel pulled him back.

'Wait Jeff, I meant nothing by it. I'm committed to you.'

Jeff studied her doubtfully.

'I promise you.'

He searched her earnest eyes, then gave the hint of a smile as the tension left his face. 'I know,' he admitted, his anger seeming to leave as fast as it had come. 'I'm sorry. I just get so, well, I don't want to lose you.'

'You won't,' Rachel assured him. 'My concern for Prince is spiritual. I want him to know God, just like I want all my friends to know God.'

But at Bible study when Rachel found herself watching the door for Prince to arrive, waiting and hoping, she wondered just what her feelings for him really were. She remembered the way he had teased her in class that morning about her 'aggressive nature' that had her in a fight with Brad Jenson. His warm, smiling eyes had made her feel alive, special, noticed. She appreciated that he cared and tried to make her feel better. But she wished she could make him understand the joy it would bring her to have him at Bible study, learning about God and sharing her faith. However, when Bible study ended and there was still no sign of him, Rachel knew it would be a miracle if he ever came.

***

Rachel was unable to participate in the school athletics carnival. The doctor cautioned her to take it easy until her broken nose was completely healed. Rachel's grandparents decided to come and watch, anyway.

112

'We might as well take this opportunity to get to know some of your friends,' Grandma said. Rachel nodded, but she knew it was more than that. Her parents had always gone along to support her in any school event and her grandparents knew that. They were trying to fill the void in her life.

Grandma and Grandpa Blythe arrived just as the carnival started, pushing baby Paul in his stroller. Rachel rushed out to meet them and lifted the smiling Paul up into her arms. She stopped his little hand as it reached for her nose, glad that her black eyes didn't seem to concern him. They were gradually fading and the doctor assured her she would look normal again soon.

'Is it safe to come near you while you're holding that little brother you're so protective of?'

Rachel turned at Prince's voice, laughing. Paul reached his chubby little hand to grab Prince's shirt sleeve and soon had it in a tight hold. Carefully, Rachel uncurled his fingers from Prince's shirt, grinning at him.

'I don't know. Are you game to try?'

Prince raised his eyes, pretending to consider, then looked back to Paul. 'I'm not sure about the big sister, but the little boy seems harmless enough. Apart from putting slobbery hands all over my shirt, anyway.'

Rachel felt love for Paul swell in her heart as he began babbling and gurgling at Prince, gazing at him with adoring eyes.

Prince moved as Paul made a lunge for his shirt again. 'What's he saying?'

'He's saying, "I love you just because you're alive and you're looking at me and you're you".'

Prince took a step backward, looking awkward. He looked almost relieved when Jeff stepped between them and took little Paul in his arms. Baby Paul forgot Prince and now concentrated on charming Jeff.

'How are you doing, buddy?' Jeff asked, swinging him into

the air. Prince moved back another step but Rachel saw the way he watched intently as Jeff played with the baby boy.

It was then that Rachel realised. Prince was afraid of babies. He didn't know what to do with them. He continued glancing in their direction every now and then but he was keeping his distance. No wonder he didn't take responsibility for the daughter people claimed he fathered.

Rachel called to him. 'Prince, come and meet my grandparents.'

For the first time ever, Rachel saw a look of shyness pass over Prince's face. Something had rattled him. However, he allowed her to lead him to the elderly couple.

'Grandma, Grandpa, this is Prince Clements.'

'Prince,' Grandpa held out his hand for the young man to shake. 'I'm George Blythe. This is my wife, Dawn.'

Prince smiled and his charming confidence returned. 'So are you the ones who taught Rachel how to fight?'

Grandpa chuckled. 'No, boy! I would have taught her how to move out of the way of a punch long ago if I knew she had this tendency to rescue little boys. Trust Rachel to have compassion on some silly kid who got into a fight way over his head.'

'Grandpa,' Rachel said, her face flaming with embarrassment. But Prince was laughing.

'That boy was my little brother.' He turned to Rachel. 'It's okay, Rachel, I'm not offended. Storm *was* in way over his head.'

Jeff joined them again, little Paul in his arms, and there was immediately an awkward silence. Jeff stared Prince down then handed Paul back to his grandmother. 'So I see you've met Kylie's ex-boyfriend; our school clown.'

Grandpa raised his eyebrows in question. 'School clown?'

'Yeah. Oh, I guess Rachel and Kylie have never mentioned that before. Prince is a bit of a performer. Always performing unbelievable and dangerous acts. He was in a circus.'

'As a clown?' Grandpa was looking between the two, and Rachel knew he had picked up the animosity between them.

'No,' Prince responded darkly, 'but Jeff wouldn't know that, since he's never bothered to try to get to know me.'

With that, he turned and stalked away. Kylie saved the moment by dancing up and throwing her arms around her grandparents.

'Grandma, Grandpa, what are you doing here? Can you come and watch me do high jump? It's my best event!'

Distracted from Prince Clements, her grandparents followed Kylie over to the high jump bars.

CHAPTER SEVENTEEN

The months flew by as teachers continued stressing the need to study and get good marks in the final exams. Rachel felt as though she were only half living. She didn't even know what she wanted to do when school was over. She had once dreamed of being a singer/songwriter or piano teacher, but though she knew she would scrape through her final piano exams, her heart wasn't in it anymore. Her grandmother suggested she see a counsellor. But there was no time for that. Besides, what if the counsellor thought she needed help? How would she fit that in between looking after baby Paul and studying for exams? It was much easier pushing memories of her parents to the back of her mind and she doubted a counsellor would let her do that.

Trial exams were fast approaching and Rachel sat at the kitchen table, struggling through her homework. Beside her, Kylie zipped and unzipped her pencil case, then leaned on the table with a sigh. When she began tapping her long fingernails in a rhythm on the back of the chair, Rachel finally looked up. Kylie gave a coy smile.

'I've been thinking, Rach, I reckon Prince is still interested in me.'

Rachel's brows rose. 'What makes you think that?'

Kylie shrugged. 'I dunno. I just feel like there's something between us, some connection I can't explain.'

'Like attraction?'

'Yeah, I guess so.'

'Do you think he feels it, too?'

Kylie laughed. 'Of course. Attraction isn't a one way game, Rachel.'

Rachel disagreed, but didn't reveal her thoughts. If she noticed Rachel's hesitation, Kylie ignored it.

'Can you find out if he still has feelings for me? I mean, since you're his friend and everything.'

Rachel frowned. 'You mean play that little game of "I know someone who likes you, do you want to know who?".'

'Of course not, silly. Just ask him if he has feelings for anyone in the class.'

'Ky, Prince and I don't talk about those kind of things.'

'Then what do you talk about?'

'Just shallow stuff, messing around and teasing, and sometimes we talk about God.'

Kylie looked surprised. 'They're two extremes, aren't they?'

'Maybe.'

'So get to know him better. Have a normal conversation with him and find out his interests, his current taste in girls.'

Rachel shrugged non-committally. Kylie had no right to believe she was attracted to Prince if she wasn't even friends enough to speak to him herself anymore.

'Please,' Kylie pleaded. Rachel's heart softened. Maybe Prince meant more to Kylie than she had realised. She let out a long, slow breath.

'Okay, I'll try.' She felt a heaviness come over her. She would speak to Prince as she said she would, but somewhere inside she knew she didn't want Prince to be attracted to her lively, outgoing cousin. Why? Maybe because somewhere deep inside she still believed dreams could come true and hidden deep within the recesses of her heart was an attraction to Prince Clements that she couldn't ignore.

Rachel forced her feet one in front of the other as she approached Prince the next day.

'How's it going?' He gave his usual smile and greeting as she sat beside him.

'Okay.'

He looked her in the eye as though searching for what was wrong. Then he sat back and stretched. 'Blaze tells me you have a new minister for your church.'

Rachel nodded, a pang of sadness hitting her. She knew the church needed a minister but having someone else stand in her father's place hurt more than she had expected.

To change the subject, she moved straight to her purpose. 'I have a friend who has feelings for you.'

Prince looked surprised but said nothing as his eyes questioned her.

'And well,' she said. 'You know who I'm talking about already, don't you?'

He shrugged. 'Maybe. I'm not sure.'

'It's Kylie.'

The corners of his mouth turned up. 'Good ol' cousin Kylie.'

'Well, I'm just wondering if I should be encouraging her feelings for you.'

Princes mouth transformed into a grin. 'That's right, you two are pretty close, aren't you?'

'Yeah.'

'So you schemed this conversation up between you.'

Rachel blushed. He saw right through it.

'It's okay.' He reached a sun-browned hand and touched her arm. 'I don't mind.'

Rachel stopped short at his touch. He hadn't touched her for a long time and it had a frightening and powerful effect on her emotions. It was so brief, less than a second, but she could still feel the sensation in the place his skin had met with hers.

You have Jeff, she reminded herself, *and you're here scheming to get Prince and your cousin back together. Most important of all, he's not a believer.*

'What are you thinking?'

Rachel was jarred back at Prince's question. She avoided answering it.

'So since you know we're schemers, what do I tell Kylie?'

He shrugged and she could tell he was amused. 'Tell her to talk to me. I like to deal with my girls in person.'

Rachel nodded, noting the way he said 'girls'. It was clear that Prince Clements was still a ladies' man.

It didn't take long for Prince and Kylie to get back together. Only the next day it became obvious the two had made up. Rachel tried not to notice the way Prince tenderly touched Kylie and gazed lovingly at her out of his dark, magnetic eyes. She walked around him passionately kissing Kylie in the corridor and felt as though she were watching a movie with a handsome hero who knew exactly the right words to say and the right way to act in a romantic love story. Except that she couldn't feel happy for the heroine if that was Kylie. At least school would soon be over. For good. But what she would do then, she had no idea.

However, as she struggled through the trial exams, she wondered if she would ever be finished with school. Once she had found study so easy but now her mind wouldn't work. Grief had somehow stolen her concentration and left her with a poor memory.

'How did you go?' Kylie asked as exam papers were handed back a week later.

Rachel felt the warmth creeping up into her face. 'I failed.'

'Which one?'

'All. Except music.'

'What?' Kylie looked as though she couldn't believe what she was hearing. 'But Rachel, you're the smart one.'

'Not anymore.'

Kylie's expression turned to one of pity. 'You've been through so much, Rach. I'm sure the teachers will let you try again.'

Rachel nodded. She had already been told she would be given exemption from these exams. Her marks would be based on her assessment over the two years of work. But how long would it take until she could think clearly again?

Jeff was more than understanding when Rachel confessed she failed her exams.

'Don't forget you're smart! And your mind *will* work normally again someday.'

'I *was* smart,' Rachel said uncertainly. 'Now I don't know.'

'Rachel, Rachel.' He took her hand. 'You still *are* smart. Sometimes I still feel intimidated by your mind.'

'Intimidated?' Rachel was shocked.

Jeff nodded. 'You're brilliant, Rachel. Don't you remember the poem you wrote me back when we were first together? Well, I've made it into a song that I sing in the nightclub.' He reached into his pocket and took out a folded sheet of paper. Rachel's eyes widened as she glanced over at it. Then she laughed and pointed. 'I hope you change that 'he' to a 'she' though, since you're the one singing it.'

His eyes shot to hers, then he laughed. 'Of course.' He quickly folded the paper up and shoved it back in his pocket. 'You could make a fortune Rachel. Someday I'll be singing all your songs in nightclubs.'

Rachel was tempted to laugh. The songs and poems she had written were not the type to be sung in nightclubs. They had way too much about God in them. It was nice of Jeff to try to make her feel better, though.

'I've been meaning to tell you I have to work full weekends now.' Jeff was studying her closely as though expecting her to be upset.

'Sunday nights too?'

Jeff nodded, looking apologetic. 'If I want to work there full time next year they want to know I'm fully committed.'

'What about Sunday mornings? Will you still come to church?

He shrugged. 'Probably not. I work late so I'll need Sunday morning to rest. The new guy isn't as good as your Dad was, anyway. Don't get me wrong, I'm still interested in God but I have different priorities now.'

Different priorities? What did that mean, exactly? If only her father were here she could talk to him about it and ask him what to do. But he wasn't here, so instead she prayed, her heart troubled and confused. At least she still had her heavenly Father, the only source of wisdom her earthly father had ever had.

CHAPTER EIGHTEEN

'You know, I let Bonnie Blake down by never sharing my faith with her,' Rachel told Jeff thoughtfully as they sat on the back verandah studying for their final music exam. Studying together once a week was the only time they had these days.

'How?' Jeff put aside his sheet of music and rested his elbows on his knees. 'Who says she would have believed anyway?'

Rachel let out a deep sigh. 'Who says she *wouldn't* have? Ever since she got burned in that fire, I've been praying for her every day, that someone will reach her and draw her to God because it's too late for me to talk to her. She's living somewhere in the city.'

Jeff frowned and began shuffling the sheaves of music at his side. 'Do you pray for many people to get to know God?'

Rachel smiled. 'Yes.' Then she gave a little laugh. 'The funny thing is, though, I never specifically prayed that you would and you're the only one who did. With you, I had to actually say something – through my song, I mean.'

He stopped shuffling the paper. 'So is it worth it?' His look was serious. 'All that time in prayer?'

Rachel nodded emphatically as she leaned her head on his shoulder. 'Even if I told everyone about Jesus, it's only God who can ever really change anyone. And prayer reminds me of that because I'm telling him what's concerning me and leaving it all with him. Even if only one person comes to believe, it's all worth it.'

Jeff sat up straighter, looking distinctly uncomfortable. 'You're not making sense. First you say that prayer isn't enough – you have to tell people about God. Then you're saying only God can make people understand so you need to pray. So which is it? Is prayer more important or is telling people about God?'

Rachel studied him. He was so logical. 'I guess both are equally important. The best thing I can do for anyone is to live completely for God, listening to him, praying for those he puts on my heart and talking to those he leads me to.' She gazed up into Jeff's eyes, letting him read all that was in her heart. 'One soul into eternal life makes me feel privileged that God has used me. It makes my life worth living even with all this pain and grief.'

'But why should your value depend on how many people come to believe the same as you? I mean, even if I didn't believe, your faith would stand on its own.'

'True.' Rachel hesitated, knowing Jeff didn't share her concern for her classmates. But he hadn't faced death like she had with her parents. Life and death wasn't an issue close to his heart. Maybe he hadn't really considered how important it was for others to live for God and go to be with him when they died. But then, she had been concerned for her classmates even before she'd lost her parents. So what was the difference between herself and Jeff?

Suddenly Jeff pulled away from her and she looked at him in surprise.

'I don't want your value and worth as a Christian to depend on me!' His tone was almost aggressive and Rachel wondered what was bothering him.

'It doesn't,' she said.

'Good. Because what would happen if I lost my faith?'

Rachel stared at him, her heart beginning to beat hard. 'Have you?' she finally asked, afraid of his answer.

'No but you haven't answered my question.'

'If you lost your faith? I guess I would pray for you and beg God to show you the truth.'

'And what if I never came back to believing? Wouldn't your prayers and everything you say then be a waste of time?'

Rachel ran a hand down her face, deep in thought. 'I'm not sure. I guess if God hadn't directed me to pray or say anything, then yes, it could be a waste of time. But would it be a waste of time to try to save a drowning person even if it looked impossible? Compassion makes me at least try.'

The two stared at one another for a moment and Rachel tried to understand the look he was giving her. He could be so intelligent and logical, but so shallow at the same time. He seemed to understand things of the Bible so quickly but there was something missing. Well, whether or not Jeff supported her she had to do her utmost to share her faith and help others get to know and love God. Even if it embarrassed and upset her boyfriend.

***

'I hope you realise the whole class is laughing about that letter you wrote,' Jeff told Rachel a few days later. He was glancing at the group huddled in the corner during study break.

Rachel's heart sank. 'What letter?'

'Some letter you wrote to Prince about how you long for him to know God. They're talking about how far they think you would go to get someone to become a Christian.' Jeff's expression told her he was angry.

'How far I'd go?'

'Yeah. Like which principles you'd be willing to break. They asked me what you gave me in return for my belief.'

Rachel blushed, understanding his meaning. 'How do they know about that letter?'

'Apparently Prince showed them.'

Distressed, Rachel began to back away from Jeff but he reached out and grabbed her arm.

'Rachel, you have to see it's not worth it. He's not going to believe and it's just making people think you have a crush on him.'

'But they know I'm committed to you.' She fought her tears. She couldn't cry; not here, not now. Jeff opened his mouth to speak but stopped when Prince came in the door.

'What's going on?'

The room fell silent. The group in the corner looked up and tried to hide what they were doing. Prince strode toward them.

'What are you doing with my folder?'

Rachel swallowed hard as Prince stormed over to the guilty-looking group. Just as he reached them, Brad held up the letter and began to read.

'If you could only see past my own poor witness and understand that God is so much more than I can show you.' Brad's voice was pleading, mocking Rachel's. *'I know I struggle to say the right words, but Prince, I –'*

Prince reached out and snatched the letter from Brad. Jeff glanced down at Rachel, gave her an 'I told you so' look and slipped out of the room. Rachel didn't even watch him go but she felt completely alone. Jeff wasn't going to support her in this.

'Where did you get this?' Prince glanced at the letter, then glared around at the group. For only a second his eyes met Rachel's but she couldn't keep looking at him. She'd never seen him this upset before and she knew her own face was flaming red.

Brad crossed his arms over his chest. 'It was on your folder, circus boy. If you don't want people reading your mail, you shouldn't leave it out for the world to see.'

Prince's eyes narrowed. 'I didn't leave it there. I've never seen it before now. So either the writer was way too careless or someone around here has been snooping through my stuff.'

Rachel didn't bother to stay and explain that she *had* put it in an envelope in Prince's locker. She escaped the room and began to search for Jeff. He had been the only one there when she put that letter in Prince's locker. A horrible thought crossed her mind. Would Jeff take it out and leave it for the class to see?

Had he decided to teach her a lesson? She shook her head. How could she think such a thing? She felt even worse when she finally found him. He stood gazing across the oval, his face a picture of anguish. He didn't even turn to look at her.

'Do you have a crush on Prince?' His voice came out hoarse. 'I know he's masculine and charming and everything, but –'

'Jeff, stop it! I told you, I'm committed to *you.*'

He turned then, and his eyes searched hers. He seemed content with what he found there. His expression lightened as he put his arm around her. 'He doesn't have enough respect for you anyway, Rachel. He proved that today, showing your letter around like that and then pretending he didn't.'

Rachel said nothing. Something still felt wrong but she decided she was being silly. What was wrong with her? Why couldn't she trust her own boyfriend?

From then, Rachel avoided Prince, embarrassed by what had happened with the letter she had written. She had longed that God would use that letter but it had backfired.

'Was I trying in my own strength?' she asked God. 'Was I not even meant to write that letter?'

Rachel wasn't sure but she decided she needed to spend more time with females. And not Kylie, for wherever Kylie was, the attractive Prince Clements would also be.

In the end, Rachel spent more time with her baby brother, ignoring Kylie's accusation that she was becoming 'an old mother'.

CHAPTER NINETEEN

Rachel was so nervous during the final exams that she didn't even respond to the way Prince kept looking her way, trying to catch her attention. She had been avoiding him quite successfully but he seemed intent on putting a stop to that, today. First he threw a piece of paper at her, then a pen. When she didn't even look up, he squeaked his shoes noisily on the floor. Still she ignored him. She couldn't deal with him right now. She had so much going through her mind she couldn't think straight. Relief filled her when the exam supervisor began handing out papers and everyone was asked to be quiet. She wished she could tell her mind the same thing. Images of her parents flashed before her eyes, causing them to fill with tears. The deep, all-consuming sadness threatened to overwhelm her and she knew that once again she would not be performing at her best. She struggled through, forcing her hand to hold the pen and form words, but knowing it would not make sense. Finally, she put down her pen and decided that would be enough.

She looked across the room to see that Prince seemed to be having the same trouble. He was shuffling in his seat, picking up the pen and putting it back down again. Finally, he ran a frustrated hand through his wavy black hair and shook his head. Something was bothering him. Deeply. He glanced her way and there was an urgency in his eyes. Slowly, Rachel raised her hand so the supervisor would come and collect her paper. Prince did the same thing. The moment she left the room, Prince's footsteps came behind her. She stopped and waited, her heart beating at the look in his eyes. Something was seriously wrong. He now stood directly before her and she saw the way he swallowed hard.

'Rachel, my brother Blaze has tetanus.'

'Tetanus?' Rachel's eyes widened. 'Wasn't he immunised?'

Prince shook his head distractedly. 'I didn't know you could be.'

Rachel had to remind herself that the Clements family were circus people. They lived in a different subculture to the average Australian citizen. But tetanus could be life threatening.

'How serious is it?'

'Very. He was having fits and now he's in a coma.'

Rachel squeezed her eyes shut. Not again. Not more grief, more death. Why wouldn't it leave her alone? She forced herself to open her eyes and look squarely at Prince. 'Is there anything I can do?'

Prince's gaze held hers, then he nodded. 'It would be good if you pray for him.'

Rachel could hardly believe her ears. Prince had asked her to pray?

'Definitely. I will.' She stood looking at him, debating whether she should give him a hug. If only she could think straight. Was it appropriate? Before she could decide, Storm's voice called Prince from the gate, where he held his brother's horse. Prince raced off, not even looking back at her.

All evening, Rachel prayed for Blaze Clements, asking God to preserve his life. She remembered the comfort the pimple-faced teenager had given her as she stood by her parents' graveside, and the anguish she read in his expression. He had loved her parents and admired them. There was a distinct possibility he could join them amongst the great cloud of witnesses any day. Once again, the reality of death engulfed her and she knew more than ever that she had to reach out to Prince and beg God to preserve his soul for eternity while there was still time. She also prayed that

God would grant Blaze Clements more time on earth to reach his family. Peace filled her and she believed with all her heart that God would do as she asked.

With shaking hands she sat at the piano and ran her hands over the keys. She still couldn't play the way she used to. Each piece she played for her exams had been mechanical and professional. But though no music was coming, the words now were. She reached for a pen and began to write, prayers and poems flowing from her heart. And in each word there was the comfort and healing she had longed for.

***

Rachel knew she would fail each exam she sat. Her mind was too full of other things.

'I never thought I'd be able to write again.' She caught Jeff as he raced off to work after their maths exam. 'But I can. It's all coming back!'

He nodded distractedly. 'I told you you would.'

'I think I'm finally healing.'

Jeff looked relieved. 'Good. Look Rach, I've got to go. They're down a few people at work and I promised I'd help out.'

Rachel nodded, watching him go. She supposed Jeff didn't care much about the exams because he was guaranteed a job at the end, anyway. Sometimes she wondered why he bothered staying on at school. He could have just started work and avoided all the stress of the exams.

'Rachel!'

She looked up, relieved Prince hadn't left yet. She was desperate to know how Blaze was.

'He's not good.' Prince looked pale and tired. 'Weird how life turns out, isn't it? Blaze is the one who's always known where he's going with life, and now it seems like God never even intended for him to grow up.'

129

Rachel shook her head. 'Don't think like that, Prince. I believe with all my heart that God will preserve Blaze's life and he will become a minister.'

'How can you say that?' Prince frowned. 'After all, God took your parents.'

Rachel nodded. 'I know. I can never say for sure, but I just have this feeling. Like I kind of had a feeling something was going to happen to my parents.'

Prince looked hard at her for a moment, then nodded. 'It was kind of creepy, wasn't it? You know, how we were talking about your parents dying, but Paul being spared. And then the next day …'

Rachel's smile was sad. 'I think God was warning me. Preparing me. But like I said, I believe Blaze will pull through. And I'm praying for him.'

Prince gave her an appreciative smile. 'Thanks.' He glanced over to where Storm stood with the horses. 'I'm thinking of selling Regal Zion.'

'What?' Rachel thought she couldn't have heard right, but Prince looked completely serious.

'Blaze got tetanus from Peter Pan. His horse. As much as Regal Zion is a part of my life, a part of me, I don't want to risk him killing me or anyone else. And what am I going to do when I finish school? I can't take a horse everywhere with me.'

Rachel swallowed hard. 'Just wait a bit, Prince. Think about it a bit more. I know how much your horse means to you.'

'My brother means more.'

Rachel wanted to cry at the defeated expression on his face. Unable to help herself, she threw her arms around him. 'It's going to be okay, Prince.'

He hugged her back. Storm called again and Rachel stepped back. 'You better go. I'll keep praying.'

He simply nodded and headed toward Storm. Even his walk looked defeated.

***

Rachel kept glancing toward Prince as she sat through her final exam. He didn't look so distracted and she hoped that was a good sign. She truly believed God would spare Blaze but wished she could pass that same confidence on to Prince.

She finished the exam and went to wait outside.

'Rachel,' Jeff greeted her. She felt a little guilty that she hadn't even noticed Jeff finish the exam and leave before her. He was looking rushed as usual. 'I just had to let you know I can't come to the formal Friday night. I've got another gig.'

'You can't make the formal?' Rachel knew the disappointment showed in her voice. Jeff was spending little time anywhere but at the nightclub these days.

'I just thought I'd let you know, since you're helping with the set up. I think we were supposed to give numbers by tonight?'

He was only letting her know because she was helping with organising? Surely he should let her know because he was her boyfriend? 'But Jeff, you only ever have one end of school formal. It's a chance to say goodbye to everyone. It's a one off opportunity.'

'I know, but one I can miss. I've never been particularly fond of school or the students.'

Rachel said nothing but wished that just for once, Jeff would think of her and come just because she wanted him to.

Jeff had been on the roster to help Rachel set up tables and seats for the formal but it was clear she would now have to find someone else. She saw Kylie come out of the exam room with Prince and approached her.

'Sorry, but no way!' Kylie told her with a laugh. 'I'm getting my hair done and I'll be pushing for time if I set up, too.'

'I'll help,' Prince offered.

Rachel looked at him in surprise. 'Thanks. I appreciate it.' She studied him. 'Any news about Blaze?'

131

'He seems to have stabilised.'

Rachel couldn't help smiling. 'Thanks God.'

He nodded. 'Yeah, thanks God.'

***

Prince arrived late to help with setting up and Rachel already had things well under way.

'Sorry I'm late,' he said, though the light in his face didn't make him look too sorry. 'I've just been at the hospital seeing Blaze, and you were right.'

'Right about what?'

'Blaze is out of danger. He's going to live!'

A smile split Rachel's face. 'I've never been more happy about being right in my life.' Every impulse wanted to throw her arms around Prince and give him a hug. She held back and the opportunity passed. She watched as Prince carried stacks of chairs into the room and then began setting them up. Jeff was taller and more solidly built than Prince but Prince had a certain charm about him that Jeff lacked. Rachel wondered if she was even attracted to Jeff. She certainly didn't feel the same way as she did now, watching Prince make his way around the room in his strong, athletic way. Prince made walking seem like a dance. His whole body seemed to flow. She found him appealing and it annoyed her. She wanted to care about people because they were people, not because they were attractive.

He caught her gaze. 'What?'

She blushed, embarrassed that he had found her gazing at him. 'Just thinking.'

'About what? My good looks?'

Rachel frowned, his arrogance catching her off guard. She answered without thought. 'The way you walk.'

'How do I walk?' He moved closer.

'Like a circus performer.'

'You mean a clown?'

132

Rachel frowned harder, thinking of Jeff's insult at the athletics carnival. 'No, like an athlete, a trapeze artist, I don't know, a dancer, maybe.'

'So you're actually complimenting me?' A slow smile formed on his handsome face.

Rachel shrugged. 'I guess so.'

'So why the dark frown?'

Her mouth twitched, though she was still too embarrassed to smile. She hadn't been aware she was frowning. She must be more careful to mask her feelings. She only hoped he hadn't noticed the open admiration she was paying him earlier. She turned away, feeling awkward. 'I don't know, but we're not here to talk. Let's work.'

He grinned at her officious manner and silently finished setting up the chairs. He didn't speak to her again until she was setting the place cards up at each table. Hers sat conspicuously alone.

'Where's Jeff's place setting?'

Rachel felt her chest tighten, painfully aware of Prince's presence by her side. 'He's not coming.'

'To our formal dinner? What's he doing that's so important?'

'He'll be out with the guys doing another gig.'

Prince gave her a strange look. 'That doesn't bother you?'

'Why should it?'

Prince shrugged and glanced around the room. 'I just think you should be careful.'

Rachel stopped what she was doing and looked directly into Prince's dark eyes. 'What do you mean?'

'Nothing.' He shoved his hands in his pockets and wouldn't meet her gaze. 'Forget I said it.'

'I can't forget it. I know what you're thinking.'

Prince's mouth tilted in the corners. 'Smart girl.'

'Is he seeing another girl?' Rachel couldn't share his amusement.

'A girl? No. But he's living a life you Christians believe is wrong.'

Rachel sighed. 'I suspected that, but I'm hoping to help him come back to God.'

'I don't think he was ever *with* God.' Prince pulled out a chair and sat down, resting his feet up on the table. 'His whole life has been an act. He uses people when it's convenient, but ...'

'An act?' Rachel asked, pushing Prince's feet off the table. Prince took on a cornered look. Rachel knew he'd gotten himself in deeper than he'd planned. He looked as though he might try to escape, but then he pulled out the chair beside him.

'Sit down.'

She glanced at her watch, then sat as he turned to face her.

'I'm talking about this gay thing.' His words came out deep and quiet as though it pained him to say it.

Rachel suddenly understood what Prince had been thinking and anger filled her. 'Jeff is not homosexual!' She sat rigid in the chair. 'You're as narrow minded as the rest of our class!'

'How do you know he's not?'

'I'm his girlfriend.'

'Yes, but has he ever slept with you? Has he even kissed you?'

Rachel's anger turned to fury. A quiet, controlled fury.

'Get away from me,' she said, her voice low and shaky. She leaned on the table and put her head in her hands, messing up the place she had just set.

'I'm just concerned,' Prince began, putting a hand on her shoulder. She flung it off.

'You're not! You've stereotyped Jeff just like everyone else has. Well, I don't want a big, tough footballer boyfriend. I want someone creative!'

'Creative? Well he's certainly creative! All his excuses and lies –'

'Get out! I've heard enough!'

Prince now smiled in amusement, clearly not intending to move. 'Rachel, I said I'd help you set up.'

'I don't want your help. Get out!'

Prince's amused look turned to one of concern as he stood, seeming to ascertain whether she meant what she said. Finally, he stood and left. Rachel watched him go, her eyes burning with tears. Why was life so complicated?

***

As Rachel tried to put on her make-up, her efforts were frustrated by the tears running down her cheeks. It was times like these she so desperately missed her parents. They weren't here to advise her on her clothing and make-up or to tell her she looked beautiful and she needed to feel beautiful tonight. Instead, she felt lost and alone. Grandpa and Grandma Blythe were wonderful, but they weren't nearly so affectionate or expressive as her parents had been.

'It's their generation,' Rachel remembered her mother explaining when as a small child she had been hurt by Grandma not wanting to cuddle her. 'They show their love in different ways.'

Now Rachel was experiencing those 'different ways'. Grandma would insist on doing everything for her – all the washing, the ironing, the cooking. And Grandpa would dole out money as though he had more than he knew what to do with. Rachel appreciated it but it simply wasn't the same.

Rachel finally arrived at the formal with a fake smile pasted on her face and no make-up. She chatted with the students around her, trying not to notice how close Prince and Kylie were sitting. Kylie looked magnificent as usual, with her wide, expressive eyes and perfect figure shown off by her tight evening dress. For the first time in months, Rachel thought of her own light brown 'lion eyes' and felt like a hurt child again.

Rachel avoided Prince's eyes throughout the meal but laughed and teased freely with Kylie. But then Brad asked Kylie to dance, and seeming flattered, Kylie left the table without even a backward glance at her boyfriend.

'The room looks good. You did a good job,' Prince said and not wanting to be rude, Rachel finally looked at him. She knew he hadn't meant to hurt her. He was a charmer but he wasn't cruel.

'I couldn't have done it without you,' she admitted, trying not to think of their disagreement that afternoon.

Prince stood and came to her side of the table. 'Dance with me?'

Rachel felt herself blushing. 'I don't know how. I've never danced before.'

He grinned. 'Well come and hold my hand while *I* dance.'

With half a smile, she took his offered hand.

His arm came to her waist and she drew in a breath, trying to control her emotions. When she managed to cast a shy glance up at him, the regret was still in his eyes.

'I'm sorry for upsetting you this afternoon, Rach. You've been such a great support to me and then I go and say something stupid and upset you.'

The way he spoke left her feeling warm somewhere inside. He was moving her amongst the dancers and she admired the smooth, skilful way his body moved with the music as though he was merely an extension of it. He made her feel as though she could dance, too.

'That's okay. I'm sorry for being oversensitive.'

'You weren't. I said some pretty awful things about Jeff. But I was just saying them because you've been such a good mate and I don't want to see you hurt.'

Rachel looked up and saw that he meant his words. It seemed he just saw her as 'one of the guys'. But was it really so bad to be considered a good friend? She found herself beginning to smile. 'I've appreciated your friendship, too. I'm going to miss you when school's finished.'

He nodded. 'I'm going to miss you, too. Especially when I have my girl troubles and need someone to talk to.'

Rachel grinned up at him. 'So you're planning to have more, are you?'

'What? Girls or troubles?'

Rachel shrugged. 'They come together in your case.'

He chuckled. 'Smart, aren't you?' Then his eyes lit up. 'Guess what? I'm all ready for uni, now. I sold Regal Zion and got a motorbike.'

So he had gone ahead and sold his horse. Rachel studied him, hoping he wouldn't regret it. To her relief, all she could see in his face was excitement.

'Prince,' she chided, 'You need a bigger vehicle than a motorbike if you want to pick up girls.'

He shook his head. 'I disagree. Bigger vehicles are more spacious. A girl has to sit right up against you on a horse or motorbike.'

Rachel couldn't help laughing at him and was about to respond when Kylie cut in. 'Can I dance with my boyfriend?' Her look was pointed and Rachel nodded and stepped back, right into Brad Jenson. Brad reached and steadied her, then took her arm. 'I guess I'd better dance with you, then.'

Rachel laughed, feeling much more lighthearted now that she and Prince had sorted things out. 'Don't feel obliged.'

'Oh but I do feel obliged,' Brad said simply. 'I mean, I have to make up for being horrible to you for so many years and for finishing it all off by breaking your nose.'

Rachel knew that, in his own way, he was apologising. 'Okay.' She gave him a grin and a shrug. 'If you put it that way.'

As they danced, Rachel realised how little she missed Jeff. If they were going to make something of their relationship, they needed to spend more time together. At the moment, the romance factor of her life was virtually non-existent, and not by her own choice. She wondered what would happen if she was accepted into university and moved away while Jeff continued with his job in the nightclub. Would they end their relationship or just continue as they always had, seeing each other if and when they had the time? Maybe it would be a relief if he just ended it. She always felt free and less tense when he wasn't around, watching her every move, suspicious every time she spoke to another male.

CHAPTER TWENTY

Rachel received her letter of acceptance into university the day before she turned eighteen. She stared down at it, unsure what to think.

What do I do, Lord? I've been accepted to study how to be a school music teacher when all I want to do is look after my little brother.

Tomorrow she would become Paul's legal guardian and yet she knew Paul wouldn't need her forever. He was growing up so fast. Every day she saw a little more of her father in the tiny, oval face with the cleft in the chin and light blond hair.

Her grandparents were supportive either way, but let her know their thoughts. 'It's up to you, Rachel,' Grandpa said, 'But we think it would be good for you to go to uni. We are very happy to continue to care for Paul until you are settled with a home or job of your own.'

Rachel didn't argue. She loved her little brother but there were times it was so obvious she wasn't ready to be a mother. She still felt in need of a mother of her own.

Still, she felt joy in the responsibility she felt when she awoke to a new day, knowing Paul was legally hers.

'You're mine, now,' she told him as she swept the giggling little boy out of his cot and into her arms. 'You always were in my heart, but now even the law says you're mine.'

***

Her deepest sadness came when she said goodbye to Kylie. Kylie had always dreamed of travelling the world and decided it was time to stop dreaming and just do it.

'You know, I never longed for a sister,' she told Rachel as they said their goodbyes. 'I always had you.'

Rachel nodded, moved by Kylie's words.

'I know we haven't been as close in the last few years,' Kylie said, 'but I've still always felt that kind of connection with you. And I always will.'

Rachel nodded again, unable to speak for the tears forming in her eyes. In saying goodbye to Kylie, she felt she was letting go of another connection to her family.

'Keep in touch,' Kylie ordered.

Rachel smiled through her tears. 'I will.'

'And stop crying or you'll have me crying, too.'

Rachel laughed, seeing that Kylie's wide, expressive eyes were already filling with uncharacteristic tears.

'Take care, my sister,' Rachel whispered, drawing Kylie into a fierce hug, then watching her leave, knowing it could be the last time they saw each other in a long time.

Jeff arrived to see Rachel not much later and he didn't seem to notice she had been crying. His walk was purposeful, his tone distant. Something was clearly on his mind.

'Rachel, we need to talk.'

Rachel sat down, concerned by the way he avoided her eyes. She heard him take a deep breath before he said, 'I think it's time we end our relationship.'

Her heart was racing but she managed to make her voice come out calm. Almost too calm. 'Why?' She had known this was a possibility and yet it still came as a shock now that it was really happening.

He shuffled uncomfortably. 'Well, we each have our own lives now. We hardly see each other anyway.'

'We could change that.'

'I'd prefer not to.'

'Okay.'

He looked directly at her then, and must have noticed that she had been crying. 'Oh Rachel, I'm sorry! This was bad timing, wasn't it?'

Rachel shrugged, trying to stop the tears which were now spilling over her eyelids. 'Not really. I'd prefer to know the truth. I mean, I don't want you to be pretending to feel something just to protect me from hurt.'

Jeff looked hard at her, a strange expression crossing over his sturdy features. 'You've been a good friend, Rachel. I couldn't have got through these last two years without you.'

Rachel was puzzled but didn't comment. Friend? Hadn't they been boyfriend and girlfriend? Hadn't they been 'in love'? True, the words had never been spoken, but Rachel had just presumed. Had she misunderstood all this time?

***

Rachel didn't tell her grandparents of her break up with Jeff, but she noticed the way they watched her. They knew something was going on. She said nothing when they expressed their gratitude that Jeff would be working in a night club not far from her university. She didn't want to take away the comfort they felt in the idea.

But as Rachel set up her new room in the residential units at university, she couldn't help thinking of Jeff. She truly missed his deep voice and serious smile, the way he so often laid a gentle hand on her shoulder. Yes, she even missed his possessive ways, because it had shown he cared. But most of all she hurt that he didn't truly love her. Not the way she had hoped and longed to be loved.

It was only a week later that Belinda from school came to visit Rachel. She seemed uncomfortable as she stood on the steps to Rachel's unit.

'I hadn't realised we were at the same uni,' she said.

Rachel smiled, inviting her in. 'It's a big uni. So how *did* you find out?'

Belinda looked even more uncomfortable as she took a seat on Rachel's tattered lounge. 'I rang your grandparents and asked where you were.'

Belinda had sought her out? Rachel was flattered that the popular girl who had once been so close to Bonnie Blake had even thought of her.

'I had something to tell you. Something I thought you should know.'

Rachel raised her eyebrows. 'About?'

'About Jeff.'

Rachel managed a small smile. 'It's okay. He broke up with me. We're not together anymore.'

Rachel thought the pronouncement would make Belinda feel better. Jeff had no obligation or connection with her any longer. However, Belinda looked more ill at ease.

'I know. I heard about it. But I thought you should know why.'

Rachel wondered what she was getting at. How would Belinda know why Jeff broke up with her? Were Belinda and Jeff now an item?

Belinda's expression showed regret and something like pity. 'I don't want to tell you, though, in case you don't believe me.'

Now Rachel was more confused than ever. 'You can tell me, Belinda.'

'No, I mean I want to show you.'

'Show me what?'

'I want you to come to a nightclub with me tonight. I know it's not your scene and you don't even have to stay.'

Rachel waited for Belinda to say more, but the girl was looking anywhere but at her. What was going on here? Could she trust Belinda? Was this some kind of set up? But why? Well, she would never know if she didn't go along.

As she entered the doors of the noisy club behind Belinda, Rachel couldn't help the butterflies that filled her stomach. She simply didn't fit here. She had never been to a place like this before.

'This way,' Belinda took Rachel's hand to lead her through the crowds. They came to a back entrance where Belinda stopped.

'Now we just have to wait.' Her eyes scanned the room, and then focussed on something. Rachel followed her gaze.

'There,' Belinda pointed and Rachel saw Jeff. However, her mind didn't comprehend it was him for a moment. He stood with his arm around another man. The man's face was scarred as though he had once been badly beaten. Rachel let out a gasp.

'Is that his cousin?'

Belinda's eyes were sad. 'It's not his cousin, Rachel. He never was.'

Rachel's heart felt as though it stopped beating. 'But he said –'

She stopped mid-sentence as Jeff bent his head and kissed the man in a manner she had only ever dreamed of being kissed. She thought she was going to vomit and her head spun.

Belinda took her arm. 'Come on, let's get out of here.' But Rachel couldn't move and neither could she avert her eyes from Jeff's face.

'Come on,' Belinda said again, and this time Rachel followed in a daze but not before Jeff had caught a glimpse of them. He bent and said something to his lover, then chased after the two girls escaping out the front door.

'Rachel! Rachel, wait!'

Dazedly, Rachel stopped.

'Do you want me here?' Belinda asked.

Rachel shook her head. 'I'll be okay.'

Belinda looked doubtful. 'Okay, I'll be waiting in the car if you need me.'

Rachel didn't watch Belinda walk away. Her gaze was fixed on the good looking young man she had once loved, who now seemed to be a total stranger. He looked down at her with both regret and pity in his expression.

'Rachel, I didn't mean for you to find out this way.'

Rachel stared at him blankly, then closed her eyes. Her voice came out in a whisper. 'Did you ever mean for me to find out?'

'I would have told you, I just wanted to wait for the right time.'

'The right time? So how long have you been …?'

'Gay? As long as I can remember.'

That wasn't what Rachel was going to ask but his words suddenly brought her to life.

'Are you sure you are, Jeff? I mean, are you *really*? You're not just giving in to all those comments people made at school?'

'Rachel.' He smiled at her pleading, reaching to place a hand on her shoulder as though she were a small child. 'I knew way before they ever suspected it. '

'But Jeff, isn't it a choice?'

The smile left his face. 'It's ironic, isn't it Rachel? I was going out with the only girl in the school who will never really understand who I am and why I'm like it.'

Rachel tried to swallow down the tears suddenly clogging her throat. 'So why did you go out with me?'

'Because I needed a girlfriend to stop the rumours. High school students are a lot less accepting of alternative lifestyles than uni students are.'

'But why me, Jeff? Why use me like that?'

'Because you're nice, Rachel and I really do like you. As a friend.' He hesitated, seeking her eyes. 'And well, I knew you wouldn't expect anything of me.'

Rachel squeezed her eyes shut, trying to ward off the confusion. When she looked at him again through blurred tears, his expression was hard. 'See what I mean? You don't even understand what I'm saying. Your principles, Rachel. They were safe.'

Then it dawned on her. Jeff knew there would be no sexual expectations. He just needed a 'girlfriend' to stop the rumours.

'You helped me to fit in at school,' he explained, 'and it got my parents off my back. But now I've come out, you're a hindrance.'

'A hindrance?'

'Gays want full commitment just like straights do. They don't want me to have a girlfriend on the side any more than you want me to have a boyfriend on the side.'

'And the boyfriend is your choice,' Rachel stated softly, resignedly, pain etched in every syllable.

'Yes. Matt is my choice.' Jeff reached to cup Rachel's face in his hands, 'But you're an amazing girl and I'll always want you for a friend.'

Rachel stepped back as though burned, the hurt and betrayal showing in her eyes. 'How can I be friends with someone who used me for so long? You pretended to love God! How can we be friends, Jeff? I don't even really know you! Our whole relationship was just an act, a convenience for you.'

Jeff stared, then laughed a loud, mocking laugh. 'Just as I thought! You have homophobia but you don't even recognise a homosexual when he's right under your nose.'

Rachel turned and ran. Once in Belinda's car, she broke into rasping sobs. 'Oh, Belinda, I'm so naïve!' Through her mind flashed the many times she had avoided male attention to appease Jeff's fears, all the times she had put other attractions aside to remain committed to the one so desperate to keep her affection. Distraught, she barely heard Belinda's attempts to comfort her. When her heart-wrenching sobs subsided, she turned red, swollen eyes to Belinda.

'Belinda, I made such fool of myself! Standing up for him when others accused him of being what he really is. I thought he loved me. I'm so stupid!'

'Rachel, stop it,' Belinda said gently. 'He doesn't deserve you. He doesn't deserve to have anyone cry over him like this.'

'Sorry.' Rachel tried to dry her tears. 'You shouldn't have to put up with me like this. It's just I've lost everything that every meant anything to me. My parents, Jeff …'

Belinda was shaking her head. 'I want to be your friend, Rachel. I always have, but you've always seemed so in control, like you didn't need or want anyone else. Now I've just seen your human side and I actually think it's possible for us to be friends.'

Rachel gazed at Belinda through her tears and saw the sincerity there. The popular, attractive Belinda who had been friends with the likes of Bonnie Blake had always wanted to be *her* friend, too? Suddenly it occurred to Rachel that not only had Jeff been acting, so had she. She had been acting as though she had no need of other people, that she had it all together, and the greatest act of all had been her belief that she was unworthy of associating with people like Belinda.

***

Once inside her unit, Rachel stared at herself in her mirror, picturing Jeff's face as he had so coldly told her the truth.

Forgive, a gentle voice inside her whispered, and Rachel nodded. *I'll try, Lord, but I need your help. I'm so angry and hurt and confused.*

Deep down, she knew her greatest fear was that this was her fault. That through her personality she had in some way asked to be so used and abused. A harsh, mocking voice began a whisper deep down inside and it grew louder and more insistent. 'You're weak, Rachel Seton. Your parents would be so ashamed. You let people walk all over you. You're naive. As if any male would really want you. You just believed Jeff loved you because you so badly wanted him to.'

Rachel sat up straighter, forcing the negative voice from her head. 'No! I am God's daughter. He gives me the strength I need. He loves me.'

Yes, God loved her and good would come from this. She was now free from Jeff. Free from his manipulative words and touch. Slowly, purposefully, she moved to her desk. Prince had tried to warn her and she had become so angry with him. How right he had been!

CHAPTER TWENTY ONE

Out of respect for Jeff Rachel had been very careful about what she said to Prince in the past. Now she could say what she liked. Prince wouldn't know about her break-up so he shouldn't read anything romantic in anything she said. She had to admit there was a bit of rebellion in her actions as she folded the poems and letters she had collated and placed them in an envelope then began on her cover note.

Dear Prince,

I have enclosed some old prayers, poems and letters for you. I didn't send them at the time I wrote them because I thought they could be taken the wrong way. Silly, I know, but as your friend I now hope you can see in them the persistent call of the loving God who couldn't let me rest until I sent them.

With love and fervent prayers,

Rachel Seton.

***

She glanced back over the poem she had written for Bonnie and Prince the night after Bonnie Blake was burned. What would have happened if she had given it to them then? If only she had. Oh well, Jeff wouldn't hold her back anymore. She didn't owe him anything. With a sigh, she sealed the envelope, then walked to the post office, sending it care of Prince's old address. She didn't even know which university he attended. As she let the parcel slide through her fingers into the post box and past the point of no return, she wondered what would come of this burden her heart was carrying. She had lectures that afternoon, but decided instead to stay home and spend some time in prayer. It seemed the more lectures she attended, the less she was convinced she was in the right place.

'What would you have me do?' she asked God, knowing he would guide her in the right direction.

Belinda came to see if she was okay. 'I was worried when I didn't see you around. Are you still upset about Jeff?'

'I'm okay.' Rachel offered her a seat and a drink. 'I'm just trying to work out what I should be doing and where I'm headed with my life.'

Belinda's look was questioning as she reached for the cup Rachel held out to her. 'You're thinking of changing courses?'

'No, I'm thinking of leaving uni altogether. Getting a job.'

'What kind of job?'

Rachel shrugged. 'Teaching kids piano, maybe.' She reached for the newspaper lying on the coffee table and handed it to Belinda. 'See this?'

Belinda read the section Rachel pointed out, then looked up at her in surprise. 'Someone in Bervale wants a piano teacher? But Rachel, it's such a tiny little town.'

Rachel nodded. 'I know. But it's close enough to the city to still have everything I need.'

'And far enough from Jeff.'

Rachel looked down, admitting that yes, she wanted to get away from Jeff. She hated the thought of running into him or his boyfriend. This place already held a lot of bad memories for her. She wanted a clean start.

'Then do it!' Belinda firmly placed her empty cup on the table. 'I'll miss you, but I admire what you're doing.'

So Rachel packed up her belongings. To her dismay, Jeff

came to see her just before she left and he was apologetic but patronising when he realised she was leaving.

'I didn't mean to be so harsh on you. I just had to say it in a way you would understand.'

Rachel wished he would just go away. He was talking as though she was clingy and needy. Her eyes narrowed. 'It's okay, I'm fine. In fact, you probably made it easier by not being nice. It made me wonder what I ever saw in you in the first place.'

He smiled and it annoyed her that he didn't take the offense she intended. 'You saw a big brother, Rachel. Admit it, that's why you never kissed me.'

Rachel's face flushed red with anger. 'I never kissed you because I didn't know how, Jeff.' She glared up at him. 'Besides, I wouldn't know if my feelings for you were feelings for a big brother. I've never had one!'

She remembered the times she had wished he would kiss her and felt sick. How could she have been so naive? 'How did you manage to act so Christian?' she demanded. 'Was all that a front, too?'

Jeff looked uncomfortable. 'Maybe I sort of believed for a while,' he confessed, 'but it's easy enough to live like a Christian. It didn't take much, really.'

Rachel shook her head, all anger draining from her. Had he truly never understood? He was still just a fellow human being in need, one who needed to know his Saviour.

'Jeff, being a Christian is about giving your life to God and living for him.'

Jeff silenced her as he held up his hand. 'Don't preach at me, Rachel. I'm not interested. And I wouldn't waste your time praying for me, either.' He glanced back the way he had come. 'I just came to apologise and make sure there's no hard feelings. I'm glad I did or I wouldn't have had the chance to say goodbye.'

When she said nothing, he bent slightly to look directly into her eyes 'So, are we all okay?'

How was she supposed to answer that? She swallowed hard. 'I'm okay, Jeff. I've got God.'

'Good. I'm glad you still have your faith.' He gave a curt nod, then turned and walked away. Rachel watched his sturdy, masculine figure retreat and shook her head. How could she have known? How could anyone know? For the first time she began to forgive herself for believing Jeff, for trusting he loved her and truly wanted to know God.

CHAPTER TWENTY TWO

It only took one advertisement in Bervale's local paper for work to start coming in. It appeared the town had been desperate for a piano teacher for years. Rachel's grandparents hired a trailer and personally brought the piano from home to put in the two bedroom rental house. Belinda helped her move in and exclaimed over the cute little home.

'I love it! It suits you, Rachel.' She looked at little Paul playing on the floor. 'It's even got room for him.'

Rachel nodded. It did. But she wasn't sure it would work to have a toddler roaming the house while she tried to teach piano.

Grandma Blythe saw her look. 'No hurry, Rachel. We love having him and will wait until you are ready. We'll bring him to see you and you can come and visit him whenever you like.'

Rachel nodded, grateful for her grandparents. She glanced around the room now containing her piano, then back to them. 'Is all this okay?'

Grandpa smiled at her. 'So you're all settled in and now you're asking our blessing?'

Rachel looked sheepish. 'I guess so.'

Grandpa's smile evaporated. 'Rachel, you are a mature and Godly young woman. We trust you. We know it can't be coincidence that you saw that ad in the paper. The job is perfect for you. Of course we'd love to have you closer, but in the end we just want you to do what God wants.'

Grateful for his support, Rachel dared give him a hug. To her surprise, he hugged her back. Tears pricked her eyes and for a moment she imagined it was her father there, filling the emptiness his death had left. It was over a year ago she had heard the awful news that changed her life but some days it still felt so fresh and raw.

Baby Paul giggled as he reached for Rachel's phone, and with a bittersweet smile, she bent and picked him up. She held him close, savouring the warmth of his little body and wishing she could have him with her always. But it just wouldn't work. Not yet. He laughed as he reached for her face and called her 'Gran'. The name brought another stab of pain to Rachel. Most children learned the name 'Mum' before they learned 'Gran'.

Rachel's first student arrived the next day. She heard the doorbell and raced to answer, expecting to see a mother with a primary school aged child. Instead she faced a woman in her early twenties with black spiked hair and tattoos on her neck and arms.

'Hi, I'm Cindy.' She suddenly looked unsure. 'I hope I'm not too early?'

Rachel managed to pull herself together. 'No, of course not. Come in.'

'Thanks so much for being willing to teach me.' Cindy dumped her handbag on the floor. 'See, my brother has a band and he said if I learn to play I can join. They already have drums, bass, and everything but they need a keyboard. So I said I'd learn. Problem is I go to uni during the week and only come home on weekends. You're the only teacher who has agreed to teach me on Saturdays.'

This was all said at full speed and Rachel found herself smiling at Cindy's enthusiasm. 'Okay, where do you want to start?'

Cindy frowned. 'Well, I know a little bit. I learned piano when I was little but I never practiced. Mum used to go crazy trying to make me. But I didn't really want to learn then. I do now.'

Rachel nodded and moved the piano seat out for Cindy. 'That makes all the difference.' She placed an easy piece of music on the piano. 'Let's start here and if it's too easy we'll move on.'

Cindy grinned as she sat down. 'I can see this is going to work. I like you already. You're the first teacher who hasn't stared at my tats and suggested I'd be better off finding someone more interested in rock music.' She began to play before Rachel could respond, but she had to admit she liked Cindy, too. There was something wild and carefree about her. Teaching Cindy was likely to be fun.

***

Rachel other students were hard work. They were more like Cindy was as a child and only came because their parents wanted them to. She looked forward to Saturday when Cindy's cheerful voice would call through her door.

'Helloooo, just me again.'

Rachel came to the door with a smile, then stopped. Today Cindy's hair was blue and styled in a lop-sided sweep across her head. Another piercing shone in her lower lip and her lacy top was covered in safety pins.

'New style,' Cindy grinned. 'Did I scare you?'

Rachel let out a laugh. 'No, but I'm glad my grandparents aren't here.'

Cindy rolled her eyes. 'You and me both. Me and oldies just don't seem to mix.' She sighed. 'And me and my boyfriends' parents never mix, either.'

Rachel pulled the piano seat out for Cindy and put the music book in front of her. 'You don't?'

Cindy's lower lip came out in a pout. 'Me and my boyfriend went to Everdeen on his Harley but the whole thing was a mess.'

Rachel sat up straighter. 'Everdeen?'

'Yeah, that's where his family is. Anyway, first his Dad disapproved of me. Said something about me being the type of girl they went to Everdeen to get away from.'

Rachel wondered whether to mention Everdeen was her home town, but Cindy was talking so fast there was no chance, anyway.

'We had a look around his old school and then he wanted to go and visit this old mate of his. I had no problem with it, but then, would you believe it, he admitted she was a girl! A girl!' Cindy looked disgusted. 'What kind of guy calls a girl his 'mate'? I would have been jealous, but then he pulled up outside this old church and I knew I had nothing to worry about. He said she was the daughter of a minister or something and she was really religious. And he told me not to tell her we're living together.'

Rachel drew in a deep breath as Cindy let out a laugh. 'Can you believe it? In this day and age, there are still people who believe it's wrong to live together? I mean, times change, society changes. But I think what stunned me most of all is that my boyfriend would care that much what a religious girl thinks of his lifestyle.'

'What's wrong with his lifestyle?' Rachel tried to sound casual. If only she had the courage to ask the name of Cindy's boyfriend but her tone and expression would be sure to make Cindy suspicious. Cindy had always referred to him as 'my boyfriend', and until now Rachel had never had any interest in finding out more.

'Wrong with it?' Cindy laughed. 'Nothing. He was a bit of a player before I tamed him but I just give him this really black look if he dares to flirt with someone and he doesn't dare cross me.'

Rachel smiled, thinking she wouldn't dare cross Cindy, either. There had to be a subtle way to ask Cindy her boyfriend's name. Her mind was still searching for options when Cindy put her hands on the piano keys and began to play with flourish. Clearly the conversation was over and Rachel had missed her chance.

It was only the next week that Rachel found out more than she ever dreamed she would. Cindy didn't call out her usual cheerful hello, but pounded on the door. Rachel took one look at her face and knew she was fuming. She stood with one hand on her hip, the other ready to continue her assault on the door.

'No music today. I just don't have it in me.'

Rachel tried not to feel nervous. She doubted she was the one Cindy was upset with, but she didn't quite know how to deal with her. 'Are you okay? What's happened?'

Cindy plonked herself in a chair and didn't even glance at the piano. 'Don't worry, I'll still pay for my lesson. You're a great listener so today I'm paying you to be my therapist.'

Rachel laughed. 'Cindy, you can just visit me and not have to pay for it. We can cancel the lesson.'

Cindy glanced around the room. 'Nah, I figure I've got more money than you. I'll pay.'

Rachel couldn't help grinning. True this house wasn't a display home, but she didn't think it was that bad. Trust Cindy to just speak her mind.

Cindy threw her handbag beside the chair and began to talk. 'I just can't believe my boyfriend! He's going to his brother's wedding and he didn't even ask me to come with him. I asked him why, and can you believe it, he said his family wouldn't approve of me. What's wrong with me, Rachel? Tell me that!'

'Nothing's wrong with you,' Rachel tried to tread carefully. 'There's nothing wrong with being individual.'

'That's right!' Cindy flung her tattooed arm in the air and Rachel tried not to smile. 'But then he admitted it's not about how I look. He doesn't want them to know we're living together! Well then, of course, I asked him what the problem was, like are they all religious or something and he said most of them are! And his brother works for a church like a minister or something! It's going to be a Christian wedding and he thinks I won't fit.' Cindy shook her head, her eyes blazing. 'Tell me, Rachel, what is so distinctly unchristian about me?'

Rachel had to swallow down a laugh. To her relief, Cindy wasn't waiting for an answer and didn't notice.

'When I got upset he tried to smooth it all over. He changed his tune and started saying Blaze and Bonnie would love and accept me just the way I am, but their wedding is not the best time for an introduction.'

Rachel drew in a sharp intake of breath, but Cindy didn't seem to notice as she continued to give details about the argument that had followed. Rachel was no longer listening. Blaze and Bonnie? Blaze Clements and Bonnie Blake? Could it be possible? Could she dare to dream that Bonnie had come to believe? The Blaze Clements she had come to know would never marry anyone unless they were a believer. And Cindy's boyfriend had to be Prince Clements. She had no doubt about that, now. If only she could ask more, but the whole situation was a bit awkward, especially since Cindy was Prince's girlfriend.

'You know what?' Cindy growled. 'I reckon he just doesn't want me to know he has a child. But I'm not stupid. I worked it out. And I'll bet you his kid will be at that wedding and instead of being man enough to confess he's got a child he's just keeping me away.'

Rachel's eyes widened. 'How do you know he's got a child?'

She gave Rachel a sly look. 'I listen to phone calls. I've heard him working out things with his brother, trying to get his brother to take the kid full time. At first I felt bad, but now I'm so glad I didn't trust him.'

'So what are you going to do?'

Cindy frowned. 'Dump him, of course. That'll teach him he can't mess with me.' She bent down and scrabbled around in her bag until she came out with her phone. 'I'll do it right now. Help me, Rachel.'

She moved from her chair to sit down beside Rachel and hold the phone screen between them. Rachel's heart beat faster. What should she do now? She couldn't help Cindy break up with Prince. Should she tell Cindy about her connection with Prince?

But Cindy was already texting on her phone. Her look was smug. 'That'll teach him. Break up by text. What sweeter revenge can there be?'

Rachel suddenly reached for the phone and grabbed it out of her hands. 'Stop!'

Cindy stared at her. 'What?'

'Have you sent it?' Rachel felt panicked.

'No. What's wrong?'

Rachel ignored the way Cindy looked at her as though she'd gone mad. 'I just think you should talk to him first. Try to work it out. Tell him why you want to go to the wedding and ask him straight out if he has a child.'

'You do?' Cindy raised her eyebrows, then began to smile. 'You're right, you know. Told you you're the best therapist I've ever had. I'll go and see him now.'

She jumped up and grinned at Rachel. 'Piano lesson over. Thanks for being a listening ear!' She walked out the door, letting it slam behind her and Rachel chuckled. At that volume it was possible the whole neighbourhood had been listening ears today.

***

When Cindy arrived the next Saturday Rachel was pleased to hear her normal cheery 'Helloooo,' coming through the door. She was smiling again and her hair was now back to black and styled more gently. Prince should even deem her 'acceptable' to take to Blaze's wedding, now.

'Looks like everything worked out well.'

Cindy nodded as she sat down on the piano stool. 'Yep. Never been happier. You're a genius, Rachel.'

'So when's the wedding?'

Cindy's response left Rachel speechless. 'I dunno and I don't care.'

'You're not going?' Rachel finally spluttered. 'I thought you were going to explain to Prince why you wanted to go.' She bit her lip when she realised she'd used his name. Cindy, however, didn't seem to notice.

'Nah, I kicked him out before the wedding.'

'You kicked him out?'

'Yeah. He had started living with me, but when he came home and said he wanted to start going to church I kicked him out. I didn't want him to start going on about me having to wear modest clothes and praying or something.'

Rachel glanced at the transparent top Cindy was wearing and once more, tried not to smile. She could imagine how people in a conservative church would react to Cindy's entrance. It would be quite entertaining.

'I talked to him like you said. Told him I knew all about his kid and everything and that he's a complete loser.'

Rachel went pale. That was not quite what she had advised.

'I can't handle a boyfriend who tells me what I can and can't do,' Cindy said. 'He's good looking and everything, but we were starting to clash too much. So my new boyfriend has moved in with me.'

A new boyfriend already? Rachel couldn't understand people like Kylie and Cindy who changed boyfriends so quickly. After her experience with Jeff, she doubted she could trust anyone again for a long time. 'What's his name?'

'His name's Pete. He's from the city and he's got an even better bike than my ex.'

Rachel was relieved. Nobody she knew. She would no longer need to watch her step when asking Cindy questions. It would make life a whole lot easier.

'At least Pete's not religious,' Cindy was saying and Rachel felt uncomfortable. She didn't want to be deceiving Cindy and she knew it was now or never. She took a deep breath.

'I'm religious,' she confessed, using Cindy's terminology and wondering what the reaction would be.

Cindy looked surprised for a moment, then smiled. 'Well at least you're nice. You're not weird or judgemental or anything.'

Rachel said nothing more, praying for more opportunities to reach out to her favourite piano student.

CHAPTER TWENTY THREE

Rachel came out of the hairdresser, shaking her head. It felt light and strange. She wasn't even sure what made her get her hair cut. It had always been long and she had never considered changing it. Maybe it was Cindy's influence. Even the hairdresser had been reluctant to cut the long, blonde curtain of hair.

'You sure? You must have been growing this forever.'

Rachel nodded. 'I'm sure.'

Now she wondered how sure she really was. It would take some getting used to. And she couldn't even show her parents and gain their reassurance. The hairdresser gushed over how wonderful it looked, but it was her parents' approval she really longed for.

She started on her grocery shopping, wishing she were not so alone. Work was enjoyable but mornings were so quiet. Most of all, she missed help with the little things. There was no one to help her decide what groceries to buy or to help her carry them to the car. It was at these times she felt most lonely, when she longed for family or someone to love. She avoided church, finding it too painful to sit and listen to a man preach and know her father would never be the one in the pulpit again. Weeks dragged by and she wondered if it was time to ask her grandparents to let Paul come and live with her. But then, what would she do with him while she taught her students? Was it fair to take him from his grandparents just to leave him alone while she taught? Most of her students were after school hours and she doubted she would find a childcare centre who would take him just for that time.

She came out of the shop, arms laden with groceries and carefully sat them beside her car while she searched through her handbag for the keys. Buying the second hand car had been another step she wished she could share with her parents. Teaching piano didn't earn a lot of money, but it was enough to provide everything she needed.

A loud vehicle raced into the spot beside her. Frowning, she looked up to see the motorbike, then stopped. She watched as the rider took off his gloves, then his helmet and turned to face her.

'Prince!' she gasped, and he let out a slow smile.

'Rachel Seton! Well, you never know who you'll come across in this part of the world.'

Rachel tried not to stare. He was as handsome and charming as ever. The only change was the small beard on his chin. It suited him, making him look more mature.

'You've done something with your hair,' he said, looking at her short and stylish cut.

She nodded, self conscious. 'I see that you have, too.'

'What? Oh, the goatee? It goes with the bike.'

She laughed. 'Yeah, mine goes with the car.'

He shook his head, letting out his familiar slow smile which deepened into a laugh. She was unable to look at him when he smiled that way.

'So what are you doing here in Bervale? I thought you were at uni.'

'No, I'm a piano teacher.'

Prince's face took on a strange expression as though something were dawning on him. 'Rachel the piano teacher.' He looked directly at her. 'Do you know Cindy Towner?'

She tried to remain casual. 'She's my favourite student.'

'She seems pretty happy with your teaching, too. She's my ex.'

Rachel let out a smile. 'Yeah, she told me.'

'What else did she tell you?' Prince now wore a worried frown.

'Nothing too bad, don't worry. So are you still living in around here?'

'Yeah. It's a nice little town and it's close enough to the city to ride there every day for uni. I've got my own place.'

Was he saying that to reassure her he wasn't living with another girl? Feeling suddenly awkward about how much Cindy had told her about him, she glanced down at her groceries. 'I've got frozen stuff in here.'

'And you have to get home.' Prince came to help her load them into the car. 'You know, I've been wanting to catch up with you.' He placed the last plastic bag neatly in her boot. 'Can I grab your phone number and come around some time?'

Rachel nodded, searching for a pen and paper in her handbag. Before she could find any, Prince had pulled a notebook and pen from his top pocket.

'I've got some handy,' he told her with an impish grin. 'Always got to be ready to give out phone numbers, you know.'

Rachel shook her head, seeing he hadn't changed much at all. He was still the womaniser he always had been. He watched as she scribbled down her details, then he put them back in his top pocket.

'Catch up with you soon.' He turned and wandered into the shop. Rachel watched him go, enjoying his strong, flowing walk. He hadn't mentioned the letter she had sent him. Maybe he hadn't received it. Maybe that was for the best.

***

Prince didn't bother to ring before visiting Rachel. He turned up unexpectedly at her door, a huge smile on his face. Rachel tried not to show how flustered she was.

'I'm just cooking tea. Have you had any?'

He shook his head. 'Nah, I was just going to pick up a hamburger or something.'

'Do you want me to put another piece of fish on? I've got plenty of veggies already cooking.'

He smiled his charming smile as he lowered himself into her lounge chair. 'That would be great!'

He sat looking around the room while Rachel put fish pieces in the oven. Then he turned to her. 'Blaze and Bonnie got married.'

Rachel couldn't help her smile of joy. 'Cindy told me. I couldn't believe it! How'd he meet up with her again?'

'Well, you wouldn't believe it.' He hesitated and grinned, 'Actually, you believe in miracles so you probably would. Bonnie became a Christian when she moved to the city. Then Blaze got given a job as a youth minister at the church she goes to. So they met up again, and well, there was always a bit of a spark between those two.'

Rachel felt tears forming in her eyes. She pulled the pot mitt from her hand and took a moment to pull herself together before facing Prince again. 'I prayed so much for Bonnie after her accident.'

Prince gave her an intense look. 'Like you prayed for me?'

So he had got her letter. She nodded, feeling awkward. Why did she become so uncomfortable when she spoke of things so close to her heart?

'I was surprised to get your poems and prayers and things.' He leaned back in the chair and she got the impression he was waiting for her to say something significant. When she didn't he spoke again. 'I've read them all. I couldn't contact you to tell you what I thought, though, because you didn't leave me an address. I had no idea where you were.'

Rachel didn't know where to look but had to know. 'So what did you think?'

His dark eyes studied her frankly. 'I don't know why you never gave me any of them when you wrote them. I had no idea what you were thinking.'

'That's what I wanted.' She blushed even as she admitted it, 'I was so scared my friendship would scare you away.'

His brows shot up. 'Why? How would it?'

'Well, it's not like I was the most popular girl in the school.'

'It's not like I was ashamed to know you.'

Rachel shrugged, looking away. 'It was just too important to me to take the risk. I care too much to want to turn you away from knowing God. And I didn't want you to think that … well, that I was just writing them because I was attracted to you just like all the other girls.'

A smile began to play about Prince's mouth. 'So you're saying you only care for me because God cares?'

'That's right. I long for you to see God's love for you and to stop fighting it.'

'So you're not attracted to me at all?' Prince stood and came to the kitchen bench beside her. His presence was disarming. Flustered, Rachel began wiping down the bench.

'Are you?' Prince pressed.

'That's irrelevant.' Rachel worked harder at wiping down the bench. His deep chuckle sounded near her ear. She stopped as his hand came over hers and he pried the cloth from her fingers.

'There's no dirt left here.' She could still hear the laughter in his voice. 'It wasn't even dirty before you started attacking it.'

Rachel felt the blush that flamed her face and she stared down at the floor. Gently, he lifted her chin until her eyes met his.

'I knew it. You *do* have feelings for me. This isn't just all about God, is it?'

'I just want you to know God, Prince. It is all about God.'

'So you're not attracted to me in any way?'

Rachel didn't answer and he chuckled. 'I knew it. You are attracted to me.'

Indignation rose up within her at the triumph in his expression. 'As if you're surprised.' She tried to turn back to the bench. 'All girls are, aren't they?'

Prince was laughing as he pulled her back toward him with

one hand, while waving the cloth in the other. 'I have the cloth. You can't wipe down the bench anymore, so let's talk.'

Rachel wanted to do anything but that, so she attempted to end the conversation with her next words.

'Prince, you can have any girl you want. I know and accept that. And you're not a Christian.'

'Perhaps,' Prince said, reaching an arm to her waist, 'but you're the only girl I've met whose love for me goes deeper than physical attraction. That means a lot to me.'

'I'm sure that's not true,' Rachel tried to pull back but he cut her off, his strong arm holding her still.

'It is. What other girl has tried to hide her feelings for me to save my soul? Now that's *real* love.'

'Prince.' She fell silent as he pulled her close against him.

'So has that old boyfriend of yours kissed you yet?' His voice was low and sultry in her ear.

'Jeff's not my boyfriend anymore.' The old shame along with overwhelming anguish shook her as she confessed the truth to Prince. 'You were right. He's a homosexual. He admitted he was using me to save face but he doesn't need me now he's come out.'

Prince could not have looked more shocked. He stepped back as though she had slapped him, his dark eyes filled with emotion. 'The jerk!' He was clearly furious as he began calling Jeff every uncharitable name he could think of.

'Prince,' Rachel pleaded and he quieted, though the fire didn't leave his dark eyes.

'So that's why he never took the opportunity to kiss you.'

He still sounded angry and Rachel cringed under his intense scrutiny. 'Jeff never kissed me because he never loved me.'

'Did you try to kiss *him?*'

'No.'

'Why not?'

'Prince, I'm not like you. I've never been kissed in my life and the truth is, I wouldn't know how.'

Prince's anger evaporated into a smile. He moved closer again and Rachel subconsciously reached for the cloth where it now lay behind him on the bench.

'Prince,' she pleaded, but this time he quieted her with a brush of his warm lips against hers. Then he pulled her close against him and his kiss deepened to become both tender and determined. When he stepped back, she stared at him, wishing her heart would slow its beating. She had experienced nothing like that before and it had left her breathless.

'The shine in your eyes has confirmed my suspicions,' Prince said with a satisfied smile. 'You enjoyed that as much as I did! You have to admit that deep inside you always knew Jeff wasn't the one for you.'

Rachel gasped. She had always dreamed of this moment. When Prince would touch and hold her this way. She had never dreamed his kiss would make her melt like that, nor his dark eyes make her so unable to think rationally or clearly. But she knew it was more trouble than it was worth. Besides, she suspected he had kissed her because he felt sorry for her. He wanted to make up for what Jeff had done.

'Prince, you and I are not on the same page. I am trying to live for God but you're living for yourself.' She reminded herself as much as him. 'I can't let this happen.'

Prince said nothing but the hurt in his eyes made Rachel want to cry.

'I can't,' she repeated. 'So please, please don't touch me again.'

He moved slowly back to the lounge and sat down. 'If that's what you want.'

His eyes were searching and Rachel swallowed hard. No, it wasn't what she wanted. Or was it? More than anything she wanted to please God and she knew that this situation she had gotten herself into was definitely not pleasing to him.

Prince stayed for tea but the meal they ate together was silent and awkward. Rachel could hardly eat for the turmoil she was feeling and her heart was heavy as she avoided looking at Prince. It wasn't until near the end that Prince spoke.

'I've been going to church.' He was watching closely for her reaction. 'Bonnie Blake was so against God but now she believes. And then my little sister, Beauty, changed so much once she gave her life to God. And with Bonnie and Blaze finding each other like Blaze asked God for all those years, well, it takes common sense to see that can't be coincidence. I still don't know what to believe but I want to find out more.'

Hope filled Rachel and she knew that her eyes were now shining more brightly than they had been when he kissed her. Was he telling the truth or did he just want to please her?

'Which church?'

'Uni church. I've been going with this guy who's doing the media course with me at uni. He's a bit quieter about his faith than Blaze ever was but he's a nice enough guy.'

'So is it good?'

Prince shrugged. 'The music's pretty cool. I reckon you'd like it.'

Rachel wanted to ask about the message. Had Prince heard about Jesus? Did he understand how much God loved him? What about sin? Did he understand that his lifestyle, living for himself and pleasure, was self-destructive? That it hurt God?

Before she could think how to ask, Prince stood. 'Well, I guess I'd better get going. And thanks for …' He gave her a mischievous smile. 'Well, everything.'

She felt the blush before it even reached her cheeks. It was alright for him to tease about the kiss. It was an everyday occurrence for him. But for her, it was a first. She needed to send him away so she could talk to God about this intense but dangerous attraction she felt. She all but pushed him out the door.

CHAPTER TWENTY FOUR

It had been weeks since Prince's visit and Rachel wondered where he was and what he was thinking. She didn't feel comfortable praying for him anymore, because every time she thought of him, the feel of his lips against hers would drown out all noble thoughts. God wouldn't be pleased but it was the only warm, comforting thought she had to dwell on.

It was late in the evening and Rachel sat alone on the lounge, feeling as though the quiet would smother her if it continued. To her relief, the phone rang and she ran to answer it, hoping it was Grandma; or better still, Prince.

'Hi Rachel. It's Jeff.'

Rachel's heart beat wildly for a few moments, but she managed to hide her disappointment and answer calmly.

'How are you, Jeff?'

'Not too bad. I got your number from Belinda. I just wanted to check you're okay.'

'Yeah, I'm okay.'

There was an awkward silence. 'That's not all.'

She waited. She wasn't going to make this easy for him. Let him say what he rang to say. 'I'm just feeling kind of bad. You've been through so much and I never wanted to add to your hurt.'

Rachel didn't answer for a moment. Any vulnerability on her part would just give him a chance to hurt her again. There was something about the familiarity of his deep voice that made her still love him and long for him. What was wrong with her?

'Is that why you didn't break up with me earlier?'

He hesitated then sighed. 'I didn't plan to carry it on so long. But your parents died and you needed me.'

Coldness seeped into Rachel's bones. 'I didn't need you, Jeff. Don't flatter yourself.'

'Didn't you? Because I can hear the resentment in your voice right now, Rachel. What would have happened if I'd told you then? When you'd just lost everything?'

'I would have felt free to spend time with my true friends, Jeff. I wouldn't have had you breathing down my neck, panicking that I might find another boyfriend and leave you back where you started with everyone knowing the truth about you.' Now that she had started she couldn't stop. 'I might have spent less hours worrying that you didn't kiss me because I wasn't pretty enough, lovable enough …'

'Rachel, stop.' His voice came out pained. 'I'm sorry. I really am. And I promise you, some guy will come along and love you one day. You'll experience a kiss way better than I could have offered.'

She didn't want his pity. How could he promise her anything? He who had deceived her for so long? She gritted her teeth. 'Thanks, Jeff, but you don't need to worry. I've experienced more than you can offer already. I'm fine.'

There was silence on the other end of the phone and Rachel felt regret begin to creep up on her. Why had she said such a thing? She had wanted to hurt him but not like that.

'I see.' Jeff now spoke quietly. 'You make out that I betrayed you when all along I was right to keep an eye on you. It was Prince, wasn't it? You're not the quiet, loyal little girlfriend you made yourself out to be. You were using me just as much as I was using you.'

Rachel shook her head. 'How dare you try to put this back on me!'

'Well, am I right?'

She didn't answer and he huffed out a sigh on the other end. 'Look Rachel, I miss you. I really do. And I love you. In a brotherly way. I just rang to say I'm sorry. Can this end here? I don't want it getting out about what happened and I'm sure you don't want me saying anything about you and Prince, either.'

Rachel drew back, so angry she could have screamed. She wished he were in front of her so she could spit on him. He had only called to make sure she wouldn't tell anyone what a fake he was? How could she long for him one moment and despise him the next?

'Just to set the record straight, I was loyal to you the whole time we were together, or whatever we were. Goodbye, Jeff. Please don't call again.' She ended the call and stood staring down at the phone. 'Oh God, I'm sorry.' A groan came from somewhere deep inside her. She paced around her small house, feeling its emptiness. Picturing her father's understanding eyes, she sank into the lounge chair and great sobs welled up from within, bursting out in loud, heart-wrenching cries. She curled up in a ball and sat huddled there for a long time. A knock came at the door but she didn't move. The knock came again. Reaching a hand to swipe at the tears she stood. She must look awful, but right now she didn't care. She needed to see someone. Anyone real and alive would do. Anyone but Jeff.

'Prince.' Rachel recognised the tall form standing in the shadowy light of her door. Her heart quickened and she knew she should be careful but she felt too tired, too sad to heed the voice within. She invited him in.

Once in the full light of the room, he studied her. 'Hey, are you okay?'

Helpless to stop them, Rachel swiped at the tears. 'Jeff rang.'

Prince's shoulders tensed as he shut the door behind him. 'What did he say?'

Rachel didn't want to see him angry. She shook her head.

'It's not really his fault. I'm just having a down day. Talking to him reminded me about losing Mum and Dad.'

To her surprise, Prince didn't seem at all uncomfortable with the way her eyes streamed with tears that flowed down her already wet cheeks. He stepped closer and took her into his arms. 'I lost my mother when I was little,' he said softly. 'I understand a little bit.'

'You did?' Rachel looked up at him, amazed at the vulnerable expression she saw on his face.

'Yeah. I hardly knew her but some days I miss her heaps. Birthdays are the worst.'

He reached a finger to wipe one of her tears and she clung to him. His hold on her made the pain seem to fade away. She felt secure and loved as he gently stroked her hair, then ran his fingers through it. One hand came to the back of her neck and began to trace the line of her jaw. Involuntarily she felt herself melting into him and longing for more. This brought her to her senses and she stepped back. This was not the same as receiving comfort from her father.

But with an appealing smile, he reached for her again. 'Come here,' he commanded softly, gently drawing her back. She allowed herself to be brought closer and raised her face to his. Gently, he kissed her mouth, then her face and neck. As his tender kisses became more urgent, she closed her eyes, wondering at the intensity of feeling she had for this man. She trusted him completely and was overwhelmed by all the new senses she was experiencing at his touch.

You're treading on dangerous ground, a voice in her heart warned, but she shook it away. She was so weary, so lonely. And Prince was everything she had ever dreamed of. She had never felt this way about anyone before. His strong hands moved over her and she felt dizzy with the emotion and desire she felt. She did not object, and by the time he led her to her bed, she had no will power left. With a sigh, she surrendered completely to his passion.

***

Rachel awoke with a start and stared at the form sleeping beside her. He looked so peaceful but she let out a cry and jumped up from the bed.

'Oh Lord, what have I done?' Silently, she dressed then slipped out of the room. She made her way to the back step where she gazed out into the dawn light. Birds were just beginning to sing and the sun was rising. Just another day, but Rachel knew her life had changed forever. She could never be the same again.

'I know you forgive, Lord,' she wept, 'but I still have to reap what I've sown.' She shook her head, horrified at her own weakness. 'Oh, what have I done?'

A quiet voice spoke somewhere deep down in her soul, reminding her of the poem she had written years ago. *His wonderful mercies are new every morning, complete and secure in every day's dawning. Never left sinking in the down of the sun, never left hidden behind all I've done.*

Even as she had written it, the meaning and hope offered in the verse from the Bible had never sunk in. Until now. God's wonderful mercies were new every morning and never had she needed those mercies as much as she did now.

'I had no idea I'm this kind of person, Lord,' she wept. 'I looked down on other people for being so weak, and now …. Please don't let this have ruined everything!'

'Rachel?'

She turned at Prince's deep, questioning voice. He stood a little behind her, witnessing her tears.

'Regrets?' he asked quietly as he studied her.

She gazed back for a few moments before answering. 'Regrets that we're not married,' she finally said. 'I've sinned.'

'Is that all?' Prince's smile was relieved as he came to her but she moved out of his reach. Having him standing so close with his shirt unbuttoned, displaying his well-toned chest was not helping anything. She averted her eyes, trying to ignore the fact that she was so attracted to him.

'It's more than that, Prince,' her voice broke, 'I've hurt my closest friend. God is my closest friend, the most important one in my life. And last night, I forgot all about Him. I put my feelings first and now I've ruined any witness I ever had to you.'

Prince frowned. 'I'm glad you forgot about God last night. The last thing I want is a woman thinking about God while I'm with her.' His mouth turned up into the smile she loved so much. 'Don't worry, I don't look down on you for giving yourself totally to me.'

'But that's the problem, Prince. I want you to see me as a holy, God-loving Christian. Someone different from you. I want you to long for what I have.'

'I do,' he declared with a lop-sided smile but her tears increased.

'Not in me!' she cried in frustration. 'In God! I want you to want a relationship with God like I have!'

'Hey, it's okay!' He came to her but once more she stepped away.

'Please don't touch me. It's so wrong.'

Prince bristled. 'How is it so wrong? Is your God really that harsh? Is it so wrong to sleep with someone you have feelings for?'

'Yes,' Rachel cried. 'I've ruined God's best plan. One woman and one man are meant to enjoy sex in marriage. Now I've put you and my feelings for you before him.' She met Prince's dark eyes, imploring him to understand. 'The first commandment is to put God first because he's a jealous God.'

Prince's expression was incredulous. 'He demands that much of you?'

'Not just of me,' Rachel swiped at her tears. 'He asks it of all of us. You too.'

'What a selfish, demanding God!' Prince put his hands on his hips and gave her a defiant look. 'If he's like that, then of course I want nothing to do with him.

'No,' Rachel contradicted quietly.

'No?'

'No, God's not selfish and demanding. He's the most unselfish person who ever lived. He wants us to put him first out of gratefulness for all he's done for us. But I think he deserves my total commitment. After all, he did give his life to save mine.'

Prince gazed at her out of dark eyes, saying nothing.

'I let him down,' Rachel whispered. 'He's forgiven me, but I hate to think I hurt him so badly.'

Hearing the emotion in her voice, Prince turned toward the door. 'Well,' he threw over his shoulder, 'I don't want to come between you and your closest friend.'

The door slammed and Rachel stared after him, knowing she had hurt him but not knowing what to do about it. She sank onto the step, feeling alone once more. But as she sat and gazed out into the morning a peace began to steal over her.

'Oh, Lord Jesus, so many years ago I asked for just one friend,' she prayed, looking into the risen sun. 'I lost my parents, my friends, my boyfriend, my witness and friendship with Prince Clements ... but I have you, Lord. I've always had you! Why couldn't I have been content with that? You are the best friend I've ever had, and I want nothing to ever come between us again!'

CHAPTER TWENTY FIVE

Rachel knew she needed to sort things out with Prince but she didn't have his address or phone number. He hadn't made any attempt to contact her, so she finally asked Cindy for his address.

'You know him?' Cindy was surprised.

Rachel had known Cindy would ask questions, but decided she would just have to answer honestly. 'Yeah. I knew him from school.'

To her surprise and relief, Cindy asked no more as she willingly wrote down the address, then handed the piece of paper to Rachel.

'You be careful,' she warned. 'He's a bit of a ladies' man and I don't want him seducing my best friend.'

'Best friend?'

'Of course,' Cindy grinned at Rachel's stunned expression. 'I've never had a friend like you before, someone who listens to all my complaints and still likes me.'

Rachel laughed, but Cindy's words warmed her heart and gave her renewed courage. She would go to see Prince that afternoon.

However, all courage failed her when she happened to run into him on her way to buy some lunch. He glanced at her, then glanced away again without another word. She wished he would talk but he made it clear he didn't want to when he walked straight past and into the newsagency. She knew she should have expected it. His relationship with Kylie should have warned her he was that type of person. He had never liked commitment or responsibility.

So Rachel left him alone but continued to pray for him.

'Are my prayers all worthless?' she asked God. 'Am I really wasting my time?'

She puzzled over and over Jesus' words of two thousand years ago. He promised that anything asked in his name would be granted.

'Surely it's your will that Prince comes to know you, Lord? Even despite my mistakes.' But she knew that God had also given Prince a free will. God never demanded love. He just asked and longed for it.

As Rachel worked through her daily anguish with prayers and tears, she felt as though each day were clouded with grief. Her heart ached constantly. And as she ached, she wrote. But still, she couldn't bring herself to sing. Instead she expressed herself in the prayers and poems which flowed from her heart and onto paper. With renewed passion and urgency, she expressed all she felt with a new depth she had never had before.

'She who is forgiven much, loves much,' she whispered, thinking of Jesus' words when he forgave the prostitute over two thousand years ago. That story had taken on a new meaning. She had also been forgiven and found a new depth in her relationship with her Saviour. She loved him with a gratitude she had never experienced before.

Finally tired, she stopped. Once again, she didn't feel well. With slow steps she made her way into the bathroom and took out the test kit she had bought from the chemist. Carefully she followed the instructions, then stood staring at the strip she held in her shaking hand. There was no doubt. She was pregnant.

'Why, Lord?' For a moment, fear claimed her. 'I don't understand. I know we reap what we sow, but should this little baby being formed inside me be so affected by my mistake?'

She thought of her grandparents. They would be so shocked, so disappointed in her. And all those who had respected her … now it would be so obvious that she had sinned. Jealousy, anger, pride – all these sins could be hidden. But a stomach swollen with child would soon be discovered. How could she ever explain it to her little brother, Paul, as he grew older? How could she be a Godly example to him now? And what about Kylie? What was she going to say to her?

'God forgives,' she said. 'But will anyone else?'

Rachel dreaded what she knew she must do. She stood outside Prince's door, gathering up the courage to knock. She had prepared herself for his denial of the situation. After all, he had refused to acknowledge he had a daughter while he was still at school.

Thoughts were racing through her mind. *What if he demands an abortion?* She knew there was no way she would even consider it. *I've brought this new little life into the world through sin, but there's no way I will selfishly destroy him or her just to make my life easier!*

It was her expression of determination Prince saw as he opened the door. She tried to speak but nothing came out. Prince studied her, then stepped aside.

'Well, hello. Come in.'

She faltered, but kept her feet firmly on the doorstep. 'Um, no thanks.'

'It's okay,' he said. 'I'm not going to pounce on you as soon as we're alone. I only come on to a girl if she gives me some kind of encouragement.'

She blushed deep red and avoided his eyes. How cheap she must seem to him.

'Hey, I'm sorry.'

He seemed genuine but Rachel had been totally thrown by his words. 'I'll ... I'll come back later,' she stuttered and rushed away, struggling to keep her tears under control.

'Wait! Rachel!' Prince rushed after her. He caught her easily but removed his hand when she jarred at his touch.

'I really am sorry.' He looked as though he was about to reach out to her again but shoved his hand in his pocket instead. Rachel looked into his apologetic eyes and shook her head. Life was so different from how she imagined it. She always wanted her children to be able to witness their parents' love and affection for one another but now, she dared not even be alone with her child's father.

'What is it? Talk to me, Rachel.' Prince's dark eyes searched hers.

'I'm pregnant.'

His eyes widened 'You are?'

'*We* are.'

Prince could not have looked more taken aback. He opened and shut his mouth a few times before he pulled himself together. He finally spoke. 'Does this mean I have to marry you?'

Now it was Rachel's turn to look shocked. After the way he had avoided her down the street after their night together, she expected at least some opposition to her announcement.

'No, no of course not. You don't have to do anything.' She looked down at her feet. 'Except, love our child.'

'But what about your faith? Don't Christians have to be married to have a child?'

'It's God's original plan. It is best,' Rachel admitted. 'But what's done is done and God's forgiven me.'

'But what will everyone think? Your grandparents? Your church?'

That had been Rachel's concern exactly but she managed a sad smile at Prince. 'They would think it just as bad if I married an unbeliever. You and I have such different goals in life, and it simply couldn't work.'

Prince squeezed his eyes shut and pinched the bridge of his nose. When he looked at her again, she knew the full implications of their thoughtless actions had hit him.

'You know I've been in this position before, don't you?'

Rachel simply nodded.

'But she wasn't a Christian. My daughter, her name is Sky. I saw her at Blaze's wedding. They say she's doing well but I really don't know. Because I hardly ever see her. I don't even think she knows I'm her father.'

Again, Rachel just nodded. Prince's shoulders slumped in defeat. 'I just don't know what to do, Rachel.'

'What do you want to do?'

Prince looked surprised at the question, as though he had expected Rachel to make all kinds of demands of him. He shrugged. 'I'll do whatever you think is best but this time I'd like to be involved.'

'I want you to be as well.' Rachel corrected herself. 'No, I need you to be.'

'I promise I'll be here for you and our child.'

Our child. They were unavoidably connected now but Rachel saw that Prince was sincere. He intended to keep his promise to be there for her.

'Please, Father God, draw Prince Clements to you!' she prayed. 'Despite my mistakes and failings. Don't hold him accountable for my sin! May he see beyond me and see you!'

CHAPTER TWENTY SIX

Rachel knew the next thing she must do was tell her grandparents. She dreaded the thought, but knew that in God's strength she could do it. As she drove the long journey back to Everdeen, she tried not to think of the devastating affect her news would have.

'Rachel!' Grandma exclaimed in pleasure as she opened the door to find her granddaughter standing there. 'Come in! I'll just go and get Paul, he's out the back.'

'No, Grandma, not yet,' Rachel followed her grandmother into the house. 'I need to talk with you and Grandpa first.'

'Oh, okay.' Her grandmother willingly led her into the lounge room where Grandpa sat reading the newspaper. He put it down, smiling in delight to see her.

Rachel knew she was shaking and her heart beat so fast she felt as though it were somewhere in her throat. But she had to say this; had to get it over with. 'Grandma, Grandpa, I just had to come and see you.' She glanced out the back door to where she could see her little brother playing in the sand pit. She longed to go to him and hold him tight but knew she must do what she came to do. The blood drained from her face and she wondered if she could go through with this.

Her grandfather pulled out a seat for her. 'Rachel, what's wrong? Sit down. Has something happened?'

Rachel lowered herself to the seat, forcing herself to look

directly into the eyes of her grandparents. No wonder Prince had been too scared to admit he had a child. Right now she would have run away and denied it if that was at all possible.

Grandma was looking at Rachel's shaking hands. 'Are you okay? You know we're here for you.'

'I know,' tears sprang to her eyes, 'but after I tell you my news, you might prefer not to be.'

Her grandmother's face paled. 'What do you mean? Rachel, what are you talking about?'

Rachel knew she had to tell them while she had the courage. 'I'm pregnant,' she blurted, then burst into tears. 'Please, please, please forgive me.'

Her grandparents took a few moments to take in the news, staring at her as though they hadn't heard right.

'Who's pregnant?'

Rachel could not look at them. 'Me. I am pregnant.'

Her grandfather jumped up. 'What happened? Were you raped? Should I call the police?'

'No, no nothing like that. No, Grandpa, it was me …'

Her grandmother shook her head as though trying to shake away what she was hearing. 'What happened?' she asked in a stunned voice.

'I don't know. I gave in to temptation. I got carried away.'

There was an absolute silence which was almost more than Rachel could bear. *Say something,* she pleaded in her mind. *Please, say something, but don't hate me.*

Finally her grandmother spoke softly, her words breaking Rachel's heart. 'You disappoint me, Rachel.'

'I know. And I disappointed myself and God.' She knew that for as long as she lived she would remember the anguish in her grandparents' faces at this moment. And she was the one who had put it there.

Her grandfather shuffled uncomfortably and cleared his throat a few times. 'Well, I hope you're going to marry him.'

'No.'

'Pardon?'

'No, I can't marry him.'

Now he looked horrified. 'Why not?'

Rachel looked down, wishing she could have just avoided her grandparents for a few years and never even told them she had a child.

'He's not a believer, Grandpa. It would just make things worse.'

'It wasn't Jeff?' her grandmother gasped.

'No. Jeff's a homosexual and has turned away from God.'

Her grandfather jumped up. 'And so you've decided to become a loose woman and turn away from God, too?' His look of anger dissolved into one of regret as Rachel broke down into heart wrenching sobs.

'I'm sorry, Rachel. Don't cry.' He came to her side. 'I didn't mean it. I'm just so shocked.'

'I know.' Rachel nodded, grief tearing at her heart. 'I deserve your anger but I need your support so badly. God has forgiven me. Can you?'

Her grandparents looked at one another and Rachel could tell they were trying to hold back their own tears. 'Oh Rachel.' Her grandmother was now weeping, 'I would have imagined this of Kylie, of anyone but you.'

Her grandfather stood, putting a protective arm around his wife. 'We love you Rachel and we will pray you through this. God's forgiven you, so we've got no right to hold it against you.'

Grandma nodded in agreement, then took in a deep, shuddering breath. 'What about the baby, Rachel? You will keep the child? You won't abort?'

Rachel was stunned that she had to ask. But then, she had slept with a man out of wedlock, something they had never expected of her. In fact, something she had never expected of herself.

'Of course,' she said. 'This child shouldn't suffer for my sin any more than is possible. I will do my best to bring him or her up to know and love our Lord.'

Both her grandparents gazed at her before drawing her into a hug where they all wept together.

'We'll be there for you as much as possible,' her grandparents said.

Rachel looked up as Paul came into the house, unaware of the conversation that had taken place. With a cry of delight, he ran to his sister's arms. Soon, in fact, within seven months, Rachel realised, she would have a child not much different in age from her little brother.

My sin has touched eternity, she realised. *This child of mine has a soul which will either reject God or accept him. This new life will exist forever.*

She gently touched her stomach and whispered down to the baby within. 'I pray with all my heart that you will believe in God and live all your days knowing and loving Him.'

***

The next person Rachel knew she needed to contact was her cousin, Prince's ex-girlfriend. Kylie was somewhere in Ireland but Grandpa was able to get a contact number from her parents. What Rachel would say she had no idea, but she knew it was important. With a prayerful heart she made the call.

An unfamiliar male voice with an Irish accent answered then called out to Kylie.

'Hey Kylie, another Aussie for you.' He chuckled and Rachel heard his muffled voice as he moved away from the phone. 'She's got a stronger accent than you do!'

'Of course, you idiot,' came back Kylie's laughing voice. 'I've been living with you Irish for a while now. I've lost my native language.' There came a few bumps as Kylie took the phone. 'Hello?'

'Kylie, it's me.'

'Rachel! I can't believe I'm hearing your voice. I've missed you so much! How are you?'

Rachel made a choice. She could make small talk or she could get straight to the point. 'Kylie, I've missed you too. But I've done something I need to tell you about.'

'Yeah?'

Kylie sounded confused, but Rachel pushed on. 'I met up with Prince Clements again. And well …'

Kylie let out a hoot of laughter. 'You're together, aren't you! I knew it, Rachel! I knew it would happen one day. Don't worry about it. I think I only really wanted him because I knew he wanted you. He always did. The way he looked at you, I just wished he would look at me that way, but he never did.'

Rachel was in shock. 'What are you talking about? I always thought the way he looked at you was special.'

'No, the way he looked at me was the way he looked at every other girl. You're the only girl he looked at with respect, Rach. You're like a sister to me and I guess I felt a bit of sibling rivalry. And don't worry, I never slept with him.'

Rachel's mind was spinning. What was Kylie saying? She didn't really have feelings for Prince, she just wanted to compete? Even so, there was more she needed to confess to her cousin.

'Kylie, I slept with him and now I'm pregnant.'

There was complete silence, then, 'What?'

'I know. I never thought I was that type of girl, but I made a mistake. It was just once. I'm sorry.'

Another silence.

'Kylie?'

'I'm in shock. I can't quite believe it, but I don't get why you're apologising to me.'

It was true Kylie had made it clear she hadn't really had any significant feelings for Prince or taken the relationship seriously, but this went a lot deeper.

'I'm sorry for not living the Christian life, for failing God, for being a hypocrite.'

'Oh Rach, you're not a hypocrite. And you're the only person on earth who would think to apologise to me for what you've done. This proves to me that you are a real human, not a perfect little saint who finds it easy to do the right thing. I used to think you mustn't have normal feelings, especially when your parents died and you just held it all together.'

Rachel felt tears sting her eyes and her voice came out hoarse. 'I didn't have it all together, Kylie. I still don't. Sorry if I made it seem that way. I'm just as human as you and without God I'd be a complete mess.'

There was a pause and when Kylie's spoke again her voice betrayed her emotion. 'I love you Rachel. And you'll get through this. I know you, and you'll do the right thing. If you need me, just say the word and I'll come straight home. I'll support you in any way I can. You're the closest thing I ever had to a sister. I'll always love you. Never forget that.'

Rachel swallowed hard. 'Thanks Kylie. I love you, too.'

***

Prince seemed just as determined to be a support as Rachel's grandparents and Kylie were. He dropped in on her and stood awkwardly outside her door. 'I think we need to spend time getting to know each other better. I need to know how I can help and how we can work as a team. I mean, we're fathering a child here.'

Rachel grinned. 'You are. I'm not.'

'What do you mean?' Prince looked baffled.

'I'll be mothering.'

Realising his mistake, he smiled slowly, but reached for her hand. 'I'm serious, Rachel.'

She pulled her hand from his. 'I know, but Prince, it's all a bit awkward. You have uni and I have my students. It's hard to find time together.'

He studied her pale face and tired lines around her eyes. Pregnancy really seemed to have taken her energy. 'Maybe we should be living together.'

In that moment Rachel knew real temptation. It would be so easy to give in to the voice that told her she had already messed up, so she might as well not be a hypocrite and allow this man to have her as he desired and as she desired.

I'm not being a hypocrite, she told herself firmly. *I'm accepting God's forgiveness and making sure I don't hurt him that way again.*

She spoke aloud. 'No, Prince. We'll have to work out some other way.'

CHAPTER TWENTY SEVEN

Rachel went to answer her door, wishing she didn't feel so tired. Her doctor assured things got better after the first three months, but her morning sickness seemed to be lasting forever.

She opened the door to see Prince standing there. His eyes shone.

'Hi Rachel, I just had to tell you, I gave my life to God.'

She stared at him, longing to believe what he had just said, but fearing to. She had been betrayed once already and Prince believing and giving his life to God seemed even more unlikely than Jeff. She didn't move from where she stood in the doorway. 'What brought this about?'

'Lots of things. I've got so much to tell you! Can I come in?'

Rachel glanced in at the empty lounge room, then back to Prince.

He held up a hand. 'Sorry, ignore that. I just thought you look tired and it's a bit awkward standing here. How about we go down to the takeaway shop and sit at those tables outside?'

She nodded, grabbed her keys to lock up behind her and fell into step beside him.

As they walked he explained. 'I've been going to uni church for a while now. I was really challenged by all your poems and so amazed that you prayed for me like you did. I just had to find out more. When I came over that night …' He glanced at her flaming face. She knew exactly the night he was speaking of. 'I was going to ask you more about God but I guess I got carried away with, well, you know.'

He had been going to ask her about God? If only she had been stronger. The regret knifed her heart and her voice came out in a whisper. 'I'm so sorry.'

He stopped mid stride. 'Okay, you've apologised but I don't want you to ever apologise for that again. You made a mistake. We both did. But God has forgiven us and turned it around for good. You believe God's forgiven you but I want you to believe I've forgiven you, too.'

She stared at him, speechless, then followed as he came to the table outside the takeaway shop and sat down. He pulled out a chair for her then moved to the other side of the table.

'Now will you forgive *me*?'

She stopped part way down into the chair. 'For what?'

'Haven't you been listening to me? You weren't the only one involved, Rachel. I instigated it, remember? And I knew you were vulnerable that night. It was totally selfish of me.'

Silently, she nodded, lowering herself down and gazing across at him.

'So will you forgive me?'

Again she nodded.

'So no more apologies from either of us.'

'Okay.' She wondered where the conversation was headed and watched as he leaned on his elbows and rested his chin in his hands. His look was intense and she couldn't pull her gaze away.

'I've known all about Jesus' death on my behalf for a long time,' he said. 'Blaze used to talk about it all the time. But I didn't want to change the way I was living. And it had never really hit my heart until, well, until last week when I was talking to a guy from uni church. It suddenly seemed to all fall into place – that this is not just some story. It's real. God really does love me, he really did die in my place. He was my substitute. He paid for all the times I messed up. And that's when I knew I was tired of living for myself the way I have been. I want a new start. And now I've asked for God's forgiveness and I have that. The old Prince has gone.'

Rachel still said nothing as she watched Prince run a hand through his black hair and sit back. 'I want our child to know God's love, too, Rachel.' He took a deep breath. 'And I don't want to only visit on weekends or when you have someone else in the house to chaperone.'

Disappointment clouded Rachel. 'Prince, you can't live with me. We're not married.'

'I know.' He swallowed hard and she saw the way he clenched his hands and rubbed his chin in a nervous way. 'But I want to change that. I know it was always God's plan for one man and one woman and I want to live the way God wants me to. If you're willing to have me, that is.'

Rachel choked on the fingernail she had been biting and Prince grinned. 'I didn't think my suggestion would get such a negative reaction.' He waited till her coughing subsided. 'Just a yes or no will do.'

She tried to gather her thoughts together. Was he really asking her to marry him? How could she know he was sincere? Could she really trust him? He was used to having any woman he wanted, so how could he be happy with just one, especially if that one was her? His eyes were imploring her to say yes but Jeff had given her that exact same look. Well, almost. Jeff's eyes had never quite drawn her in, made her melt somewhere inside the way Prince's did. She prayed for wisdom, then reached a hand toward him. 'What about a "wait"?'

'Wait until what?' He took the hand she held out to him. 'I want to be there when our little one is born.'

Rachel couldn't bring herself to confess her fears. She didn't want to hurt him that way but his eyes suddenly widened in understanding. 'You need to know that I mean it, don't you?' His hand tightened around hers. 'You don't want a husband who says he's a Christian so he can marry you. You've already been burned by a guy who pretended to be a Christian.'

She nodded, not admitting that she also needed to know Prince loved her. She desperately wanted her baby to have a father but all her life she had dreamed of being loved deeply and completely by a man; her husband. She didn't think she could bear the thought of a marriage without that love.

Prince didn't pressure Rachel but he insisted on spending time with her. She always suggested a public place and he agreed without protest.

'I have my first ultrasound tomorrow,' Rachel said one evening as they sat at the tables outside the takeaway shop. Once again, they were swiping at mosquitoes but Prince never complained.

'Is that like an x-ray of the baby?' Prince slapped at his arm and flicked the dead mosquito onto the ground while Rachel smiled at his ignorance.

'Kind of, but you can see everything live on the computer screen.'

'So you will see our baby?'

'Maybe. I've been told that sometimes you can't, because you're lying down beside the screen. The nurse will be able to see, though.'

'Will they tell you if it's a boy or girl?'

'Only if I ask.'

'I think you should ask.' He reached out and took her hand and she smiled at his enthusiasm, covering his hand with her own. She was beginning to understand that Prince was not being seductive every time he touched her. He was merely an affectionate person like her father had been.

'You want to know what we're having?'

He grinned. 'I'm presuming we're having a baby.' Then his

teasing look faded. 'I'd like to know if we're having a boy or girl.' He came to her and placed a gentle hand on her growing stomach. Regret shadowed his handsome face. 'I missed this with Sky. I was too scared to even admit I was a father. It was just too big a thing for me at sixteen.'

Rachel nodded. 'We're still children at sixteen. But then, I still feel like such a child sometimes.'

Prince studied her, his head on the side. 'Are you scared?'

'Terrified. Sometimes I feel so alone.'

He drew her close and the tenderness in his expression touched her somewhere deep inside. 'I don't want you to be alone, Rachel. Not ever again.'

Rachel gazed up at him. Prince Clements had changed. No longer did he shower his charms on her in a seductive way, yet his gentle, caring nature made him all the more appealing. He smiled at her, asking what she was thinking, but she was unwilling to share. He looked at her for a few moments, then spoke. 'There's something I've been wanting to ask you.'

'Ask away.'

He bit his lip and hesitated. 'Well, our church needs someone to play the piano in the evening service. I told them about you. I wondered if you'd be willing.'

Rachel laughed, 'But I won't even be able to fit behind a piano soon.'

He raised an eyebrow and she knew he didn't believe her. 'It's not just that,' he confessed. 'Sometimes I just so badly wish you were there hearing what I'm hearing, able to discuss the sermons with me. I want to be able to share it with you. I want to talk about more than our baby.'

Rachel saw the yearning in his eyes and her heart leaped. She hadn't been back to church since finding out she was pregnant. Although she knew God had forgiven her, she hadn't been able to bring herself to face his people. And something about being in a church brought back so many memories of her parents she felt like she was suffocating with the grief that would suddenly overwhelm her.

'Do they know about me? About us?' Rachel longed to spend time with God's people, hearing his word again, but not if she had to explain her situation to them all.

'I've told some of them.' Prince reached to gently brush a mosquito from her face. 'I don't think they'll condemn you if that's what you're worried about. They were pretty understanding and supportive with me.'

Rachel smiled ruefully. 'Yeah, but you weren't a Christian when it happened.'

'No,' he agreed, 'but I was human, just like you are. If God forgives sinners, how much more will he forgive his own children when they ask for it?'

Rachel's eyes filled with tears. 'I've made such mistakes, though. I'm no different from – no, I'm even worse than some of the people who don't even believe in God.'

'Except you're forgiven.' Prince reminded her. 'Which is what this whole Christianity thing is about, as I understand it. God forgiving us for not being able to meet his standards.'

'But then I'm supposed to try to live the way he wants,' Rachel argued. 'With his help, of course.'

'Exactly.' Prince smiled. 'Don't you think God wants us to accept his forgiveness when we fail? Doesn't he want us to live without guilt? Forgiven people are the only ones who *should* be living without guilt. Not because they don't make mistakes but because those mistakes aren't counted against them.'

Rachel caught her breath at his words. She had never dreamed she would see Prince Clements like this. He understood so much more about God than she ever thought possible.

He grinned at her. 'And yes, I did learn all that at church. And everyone else there has been hearing the exact same sermons, so if they've taken it to heart you'll be fine.'

'I'll come to uni church with you,' she relented, 'and yes, I'll play the piano for as long as I can fit on the stool. I've been missing playing the piano.'

Prince's smile was delighted as he gave her an impulsive hug. She was both disappointed and relieved when he quickly let her go again. She would so love to be married to this man. But was it God's best plan? She didn't want to put her emotions and desires above God's best plan ever again.

CHAPTER TWENTY EIGHT

Rachel couldn't help shaking as she lay on the bed beside the computer screen the next morning. The sonographer bustled around the room, then smiled at Rachel.

'Your first child?'

'Yes.' Rachel hoped the sonographer wouldn't ask if she was married. She would feel so ashamed to have to confess she wasn't. She watched the woman squeeze gel onto the end of the instrument and gathered up her courage. 'Um, I'd like to know what gender the baby is.'

The sonographer nodded as she moved the cool gel across Rachel's swollen abdomen. Then she stopped and looked hard at the screen before turning to Rachel with a smile.'Which one do you want to know first?'

'Pardon?' Rachel tried to see the screen.

'You have twins here, Rachel.'

'I have what?'

The lady chuckled at Rachel's disbelieving look. 'Twins. I can see straight away that one is a little boy –'

As she spoke, there came a knock at the door, but Rachel didn't notice. She was in shock.

'Come in.'

Rachel looked to the door, and her heart fluttered as Prince himself stepped in the room. His dark eyes scanned the room, then locked with hers.

'Prince!' She fell back onto the bed with relief.

'I had to come.' He gave her a tender, apologetic smile, then lowered himself into the seat beside her. 'I hope you don't mind.' His hand reached for hers and she grasped his warm, strong fingers.

'I'm glad you came,' she whispered, knowing her hand was clammy with sweat but not wanting to let go.

Dread filled his eyes for an instant. 'Why, what's wrong?'

The sonographer spoke first. 'Nothing's wrong. You're having twins. A little boy … and here, I can now see that this one's a little girl. Both strong and healthy.'

'Twins?' Prince looked to Rachel for confirmation, then smiled in delight and squeezed her hand. But Rachel wasn't so delighted.

What do I do now, Lord? She watched Prince squint at the screen, trying to make out the forms of his children. *If it was only one, I might have been able to manage on my own. But two? I need help, but I don't want to move in with Grandma and Grandpa. I want Prince to be nearby.*

Suddenly it was clear. The wise thing would be to marry Prince Clements.

'Who would have imagined?' There was an added spring in Prince's step as they left the hospital together, a copy of the ultra sound picture in Prince's top pocket. 'Two!'

'I guess it makes sense,' Rachel said, not sharing Prince's excitement. 'After all, you're a triplet, my parents had twins.'

Prince stopped. 'Your parents had twins?'

Rachel frowned, realising she had never told him. 'Paul was a twin. Mum lost his sister earlier in the pregancy.'

Prince swallowed hard, pulling Rachel against him. 'You've been through so much! And now I'm putting you through more.'

His voice was husky and Rachel pulled away. 'Prince, it's okay. Really. Remember we weren't going to feel guilt anymore? All is forgiven.'

'I know. Sorry.' His look was sheepish as he pulled himself

together and stood tall. He shook his head with a smile. 'When I met you all those years ago at school, I never thought I'd end up feeling for you this way. Rachel, whatever happens, I'm going to do my best to be here for you.'

He felt for her. Felt what exactly? Compassion, concern … but could he ever love her? Rachel knew that love or no love, she would have to ask him what was heavy on her heart. She waited until they were getting in the car.

'Prince, you know how you said you thought it would be best if we were married?'

He lowered himself into the car and studied her. 'Yeah?'

'Well I think you were right.' She started the engine, looking ahead at the road and waiting for him to shut his door. 'I mean, now that we're having twins. I'm going to need your help so much!'

Rachel was busy steering the car out of the car park and so only caught a glimpse of his delighted smile out the corner of her eye.

'So you're saying yes to my proposal, while you're driving, when I can't even give you a hug or swing you around in my arms and kiss the living daylights out of you?'

Rachel felt a blush coming to her cheeks and glanced his way.

'I need you, Prince. For the twins.'

'Rachel, pull over for a minute, would you?'

Rachel glanced at him again, concerned by the way the smile had evaporated from his face. He looked so serious. Taking a deep breath, she pulled over. He waited for her to look at him, then undid his seatbelt and turned to directly face her.

'Okay, so you're agreeing to marry me for the twins, right?'

Rachel nodded.

'And because it wouldn't look right if I were living in your home helping you and we weren't married. People might think we were being intimate. Right?'

Again, she nodded and he took her hands in his. 'Well, Rach, I'm sorry, but I don't want to marry you unless you love me. And

I don't want to marry you unless we can sleep together. The truth is, I don't think I'd be able to help myself. I don't think you have any idea just how attractive you are.'

Rachel's eyes widened and her blush deepened. So there it was. He was attracted to her. But did he love her? Truly love her, the way she was deep down inside?

'Okay,' she whispered and restarted the car. 'I want a real marriage, too.'

He stopped her hand before it released the handbrake. 'But I need to know, do you love me?'

She bit her lip and forced herself to look at him. 'Yes, Prince, I love you. And not just with God's love. I love you in every way possible.'

His eyes looked deep into hers as though trying to find confirmation there. Rachel presumed he had found it when he sat back and let her release the handbrake.

'So when do we get married? How?'

She glanced at him before moving back onto the road. 'Soon? I want to get *some* wedding photos and I don't want to be looking too huge. They say between three and six months of pregnancy you feel the best.'

'So I'll find out what it involves, get the paper work sorted out.' Prince hesitated. 'Who do we get to marry us?'

She shrugged. 'I don't care what minister we pick. If my Dad can't be there …' Her voice broke and Prince laid a comforting hand on hers.

'What about my minister? He was the one who brought me to know God and it would be kind of special.'

'Fine.'

'And what about guests, all that stuff?'

Rachel frowned. 'I don't feel right asking my grandparents to pay for a wedding. Can we just have us and our immediate families?'

Even as Rachel spoke the words, she knew this wedding was

going to be nothing like she had dreamed as a little girl. For a start, her father would not be there to walk her down the aisle. And here she was talking with her future husband about their wedding as though they were discussing a business transaction. She knew that as she repeated the wedding vows, she would not know for sure whether the man before her really loved her or whether he was merely concerned for the two children inside her womb. He admitted he was attracted to her but the Prince she had known through high school was attracted to any and every woman. She was too scared to ask him if he loved her because she didn't know if she could cope if the answer was no.

They approached Rachel's front door and Prince suddenly stopped, looking uncomfortable. 'Do I have to propose to you?'

She grinned. 'You already did, kind of. I choked on my fingernail, remember?'

He grinned too and reached for her hand. 'So you're really my fiancée?'

'I guess so.'

He smiled wide. 'And soon we'll be married.'

She nodded and he reached a hand to touch her hair. She tensed as his dark head moved toward hers and she felt his breath on her cheek. However, he stopped just short of her mouth and searched her eyes. 'You tell me when you're comfortable with this. I don't want to rush you.'

Rachel blushed, unable to speak. Everything was happening too fast. When would she stop feeling overwhelmed and be able to respond to Prince, showing him all she felt?

His hand dropped from her hair. 'Well, I'd better get back to uni. Give me a call when you're ready to talk again.'

Rachel watched him walk away, then went inside to make a phone call. There was so much to do and so little time. First, she needed to talk to her grandparents.

CHAPTER TWENTY NINE

As Rachel entered the uni church that Sunday evening with Prince by her side, some of her fears dissipated. This building looked nothing like any of the quaint old buildings her father had preached in. This looked more like the school auditorium.

She felt Prince tighten his hold on her hand and smiled up at him. She never imagined this could really happen. Here she was, walking into church holding Prince Clements' hand. And yet there was a deep sadness in the knowledge of how it had all come about.

A well-dressed man in his late forties headed their way and Prince moved eagerly forward. 'Alan, this is my fiancée, Rachel. Rachel, this is Alan, my minister.'

'Fiancée?' Alan asked with a wide, friendly smile. 'Since when?'

'Wednesday.'

Alan smiled wider and shook Rachel's hand warmly. Despite the warmth in his welcome, Rachel saw the way he studied her. What did he know? Could he see that deep inside she felt like a broken flower beginning to wilt?

'Congratulations.' He focused his attention on Rachel. 'It's so good to have you here, Rachel. And not just because you're interested in joining our music team. It's been a real privilege to get to know Prince and an honour to meet the person who led him to know God.'

Rachel frowned in puzzlement. 'I didn't …'

She stopped at the look Prince gave her. 'You did,' he said

quietly. 'Alan only led me through the final step. There's a lot more to believing than finally admitting you do.'

Rachel had no response and was grateful when Alan changed the subject.

'I hear you write songs.'

Rachel smiled. 'Well, I used to. I haven't for a while.'

'We'd love to hear them. That's if you're willing.'

Before Rachel could answer, Alan was pulled away by the church secretary. Rachel stared after him, looking stricken. Prince leaned down and whispered in her ear.

'What's wrong?'

'I don't know. I just feel like such a hypocrite being here. Like everyone thinks I'm a good Christian who led my fiancé to know God. But the reality is …'

Prince stopped her with a hand to her mouth. 'Don't say it. You made a mistake. A mistake you are forgiven for. What about all those years you lived every moment for God, praying, loving? What about all those heartfelt poems you wrote for me? Do you really think any person here is really any better or worse than you?'

As Rachel looked into his warm, magnetic eyes it occurred to her that he was right. The Christian life wasn't about what she had and hadn't done. It wasn't about being 'good' or 'bad'. It was all about the fact that God had mercy on her and sent Jesus to forgive. She had known it, theoretically, for so many years. And now, suddenly, it was beginning to sink in. It was what Prince had been trying to tell her for weeks now. She straightened her shoulders and stood taller. He grinned at her. 'That's better.'

She grinned back, and by the time Prince's university friends came to meet her, she stood with poise and confidence, smiling at them in a way that explained why Prince Clements had chosen such a woman to be his wife.

Alan was delighted to be asked to conduct Prince and Rachel's wedding, and agreed that the sooner they were married, the better. However, he did insist upon taking them through marriage counselling, first.

At first Rachel felt uncomfortable but she could see the benefits of learning to communicate with one another openly and honestly before marriage. Alan had a way about him that helped her relax, and Prince seemed to thoroughly enjoy the time. He had no reservations about sharing his deepest feelings. During one of the sessions he told her all about his daughter, Sky.

'Her mother was even younger than I was when she was conceived and she couldn't cope with her,' he revealed. 'She had a bit of a drinking problem, which I knew but tried to ignore. I had no idea how to be a father, so I refused to even admit Sky was mine, though everyone knew she was. My brother, Blaze, now has guardianship of her, but when she's older I'd like to give her the choice of becoming a part of our family.'

When Rachel had no response, Alan turned to her. 'Would it bother you if she were part of your family?'

Rachel swallowed deeply, then looked at Prince, her heart beating hard against her chest and tears threatening. There was so much she hadn't told Prince, so much that might make him change his mind.

'First, you should know I also have guardianship of a child.' She wrung her hands together. 'My little brother is under my care. I had been thinking it was time to take on the responsibility before … just before I found out I was expecting.'

'*We*.' Prince corrected her. '*We* are expecting, Rachel.'

'Sorry, *we*. And I'm so sorry I didn't tell you about Paul before.'

Prince shook his head. 'No need to be sorry. There was no reason to tell me about him. You're always apologising, Rachel.'

'Sorry,' she began, then stopped short, realising how chronic her problem really was. She giggled but Prince shook his head in frustration.

'Rachel, you've apologised so much. For our choice

to sleep together, for not being a better Christian, for any misunderstandings. You might as well apologise for being born.'

Rachel bit her lip, stung by his words. Then a surprising anger filled her. It was alright for him. He didn't have reason to feel the shame and guilt she did. He didn't have the insecurities, the pain.

'The truth is, I am sorry for being alive.' Her eyes challenged him. 'And I have good reason to be sorry. I'm sorry that it's me sitting here and not my parents. They had such an natural way of sharing God with people. They knew so much, loved so much, when all I could do was pray. So many times I've wished it were them who were here to take care of Paul. Instead there's just me who will only have two children born out of wedlock to show him as an example of Christian living. Yes, I wish God had taken me.'

In one bound, Prince was by her side, taking her into her arms. 'Oh Rachel, don't.' His voice was pleading. 'Don't talk that way. I can't stand the thought of you not being here.'

'Really?' She raised tear-filled eyes to his. 'You don't think it would have been easier not to have gone through any of this?'

'Of course it would have been easier, but never existing would have been easier, too, wouldn't it?'

'Yes.'

'But then we would never have known the joy of living, breathing, knowing God. And if you had died instead of your parents, you never would have sent me all those poems. You never would have been there at school to be an example to me of how to live for God. And most of all, you wouldn't have prayed for me like you have all this time.'

Rachel's smile was watery but filled with hope. It was true. God really *could* use anyone. Mistakes and all. And he had used her to reach out to Prince Clements. 'You know, I once asked my Dad if he thought all my prayers were useless if my life didn't match up to them,' she said. 'Now I know they weren't. God looks at the heart.'

'He does,' the minister agreed, cutting in, though Rachel had forgotten he was even there. 'Appearance doesn't matter, Rachel. Always remember that. It doesn't matter what other people think. It's what God thinks that matters.'

At his words, Rachel remembered her mother saying exactly the same thing. And ironically, Jeff had, too. With a hesitant smile, she turned to Prince. 'One more apology?'

He frowned.

'Please.'

He shrugged. 'If that's a promise. The last one.'

Rachel reached over and took his hand, gazing directly into his dark eyes. She saw a depth there she had never noticed before. 'Prince, I'm sorry for forgetting I am adopted as a child of God.' She licked suddenly dry lips. 'For always thinking I'm unworthy because of my lion eyes, my plain hair, my reserved ways, my failure to live for God. From now on I am going to live as the princess I am and I want you to hold me accountable.'

He smiled slowly, then reached over to draw her into a hug. 'You've got a deal, Rachel Seton.' His look turned mischievous. 'Rachel Seton. I have to use your full name while I can, because you won't have it much longer.'

Watching them, Alan smiled. 'I have to admit I was a bit concerned when I first started counselling you two.'

Prince grinned. 'What, and now you're very concerned?'

Alan chuckled. 'No, actually. I'm deeply moved. I've learned how God truly can bring about release and healing. How he can and does turn everything around for good for those who love Him.'

'Romans 8:28,' Rachel quoted. One of her father's favourite verses.

Alan nodded. 'Exactly. And Rachel, I've learned a valuable lesson. I will never again judge so harshly a child of God who has fallen into sin. I see in you a beautiful, Godly woman who made one costly mistake. It could happen to anyone. It could happen to me.'

Rachel nodded. It was so true. She never dreamed she would fall so far, nor that God would so openly forgive and renew his blessings.

CHAPTER THIRTY

Prince and Rachel travelled home in Rachel's car, both deep in thought. Neither said anything until they had pulled up outside Rachel's home. She reached to open the door when Prince grabbed her hand.

'You didn't end up answering my question about Sky.' His eyes were probing. 'You didn't say how you would feel if she lived with us some time down the track.'

'You're right. I didn't.' Rachel gave him a cheeky grin as she moved to open the door. Before she could, he leaned across her and pushed down the central locking. He didn't move back to his side but looked deep into her eyes.

'How am I going to put up with you, Rachel Seton?' he asked in a low, warm voice. 'One minute you're crying all over me and the next you're teasing me when I'm trying to be serious.'

Her lips twitched. 'You trying to back out of this marriage thing?'

'No. But you're not leaving this car until I get an answer.'

'Fine,' Rachel chuckled. 'We'll just have to spend the night in here.'

He gave her a look. 'People might talk, you know.'

With horror, she realised the implications of what she had said. She opened her mouth to apologise, then saw the look on Prince's face. It was part amusement, part challenge. He knew she had been going to apologise.

'What?' She lifted her chin defensively.

'You are amazing.' His face moved closer. She stiffened and spoke quickly.

'In answer to your question, I would love to meet Sky and have no problem with her living with us.' She unlocked her door and stepped out of the car. 'But as Alan said, we might need to get to know each other as husband and wife first. It's going to be harder for us because of our situation.'

Prince stepped out of the car too, but rather than go to his motorbike, he followed her down the path. While she fumbled with her keys, Prince stepped between her and the door. Her eyes questioned him and he took a step closer. Then he moved his hand to push a strand of hair from her face. The tenderness in his expression stopped her breathing for a moment. This time she couldn't step back; couldn't move.

'I love your lion eyes.' His voice was deep. 'And I love your hair. There's nothing plain about you.'

She smiled rather tentatively. 'Prince ...'

'Princess?'

She fell silent, forgetting what she had been going to say. It was true. Pregnant or not. Sinful or not. She was the daughter of the King of kings. The King of the universe. The thought gave her boldness, and she reached to put her arms around Prince's neck. Then gently, hesitantly, she brushed her mouth against his. She felt rather than heard him draw in his breath as his arms came around her.

'Thank you, God,' she heard him whisper before he bent his head and kissed her deeply. When she pulled back, his look was serious.

'Perhaps we shouldn't do that again until we're married.'

She nodded. 'It's only a few weeks away, anyway.'

He smiled, stepping out of her way so she could unlock her door. 'It seems a long way away to me.'

***

Prince and Rachel attended birth classes together the following week, and Rachel was amused by Prince's enthusiasm.

'Well, I have to make up for missing out on Sky's early years,' he said as he volunteered to change the nappy on a doll. Rachel was aware of every other woman's envious eyes on Prince as he stood and placed the nappy expertly around the doll.

The midwife smiled at him. 'Very good for a beginner. You sure you haven't done this before?'

'Yes.' He shot Rachel a look. 'And I'm never doing it again.'

The group of women booed and chastised him while Rachel merely grinned. He was a good sport, really. He sat close as the group watched a video on labor and birth. Rachel became tense and squeezed Prince's hand a bit tighter every time a new stage was shown. Prince didn't seem bothered and she caught him grinning at her each time she squeezed his hand. When it was finally over, she relaxed, wondering what Prince thought of it all. Was he as frightened as she was? Did all the blood bother him?

He led her toward the cafeteria. 'Let's get a coffee before we head home.'

'You need time to recover?' Her tone was playful but she really wanted to know.

'Nah, I'm fine with it. But I must admit there's nothing romantic about birth.'

'And there's nothing romantic about dirty nappies or baby sick, either, so if you're marrying me for the romance, you'd better back out now.'

'You know I'm not,' he drew her close to his side. 'I've had enough of romance. Time to live in reality and face my responsibilities.' He caught her look. 'What?'

She focussed on her feet and shrugged. 'I guess I'm just hoping you won't give up romance totally.'

204

He kissed her hair. 'How could I?'

She smiled shyly up at him, then turned serious. 'Prince, what if you find yourself comparing me with all those other girls you've had? What if I don't match up?'

He touched a finger to her cheek. 'You, Rachel Seton, have surpassed them all already.'

At her doubtful look he stopped. 'It's true, Rach. Do you find yourself comparing me with Jeff?'

'To Jeff? How could I?'

He smiled. 'Aha, so you do understand.' His smile faded. 'To tell you the truth, Rachel, I feel like for the first time in my life I've found love much deeper than emotion and desire. And I've found what a joy it can be to give and expect nothing in return.'

Rachel found herself smiling as joy brimmed in her heart. He hadn't directly said he loved her but it was pretty close.

***

Wedding preparations brought Prince and Rachel together a lot more and Rachel's loneliness disappeared. It felt good to work with someone, to plan together.

Rachel watched Prince as he frowned over the guest list. 'Are you going to ask Sky to the wedding?'

Prince shook his head. 'I think not.' He twirled the pen around in his nimble fingers with amazing speed and agility. Distracted, Rachel watched until Prince followed her gaze and put the pen down. It was the kind of thing he did without thought, and once more Rachel was reminded how unusual and gifted he was. Prince began tapping his fingers on the table. 'It's not that I don't want her there. I really want to get to know her better. It's just it's not really the appropriate time, now that she's old enough to understand that I'm her father.'

'Does she know you are?'

Prince nodded. 'I think so. When I met her at Blaze and

205

Bonnie's wedding, I gave her a photo of me and told her who I am. I don't think she understood, but Blaze said he would explain.' He smiled ruefully. 'I don't think I gave her much chance of understanding. I was so nervous I spoke really fast, then disappeared as fast as I could.'

Rachel nodded, then had an idea. 'Why don't you write her a letter or something with the invitation to Blaze and Bonnie? Tell her you'd rather spend time with her when there's not so many people around.'

'You mean you and I go and visit her soon?' Prince's eyes lit up. 'It would be so much easier to talk with Sky with you there, too. I've seen you with your little brother and you're a bit of an expert with children.'

Rachel smiled at his compliment. Having a little brother had given her a lot of experience, but she had always liked children. 'I'd love to come with you,' she said. 'Promise Sky it will be soon. Little children cling to promises like that. It will make her realise she's not being rejected and that she's special to you.'

Prince tore a blank piece of paper out of the book he had been writing the guest list in. He picked up the pen and sat poised, grinning at Rachel. 'Okay, begin dictating.'

She shook her head and grinned back. 'Hey, no. You have to write it. I'm happy to help, but it has to be from you.'

He threw her a mock pout. 'Oh. I was all keen to write my little girl a poetic letter she'll treasure for always.'

Rachel chuckled at him. 'So do it. I reckon anyone can be poetic if they want to be. Especially when they're writing from the heart.'

Prince studied her for a moment, then bent his dark head over the paper and began to write. Rachel prayed for him as she always had. This time she prayed for wisdom and the words he needed to express to the daughter he hardly knew.

CHAPTER THIRTY ONE

Butterflies fluttered inside Rachel as her grandmother fussed with her wedding dress. The day had come but it was not how she had dreamed. She was pregnant. And her mother and father weren't here. She wanted to weep but held herself together. Grandma Blythe wouldn't know what to do with a weeping bride.

Finally, Grandma Blythe stood back and her eyes became moist. 'You look beautiful!' She drew Rachel into an unexpected hug. 'I know it's been hard, Rachel,' she said softly, 'but you've come through all of this in a way that's made me proud. Your strength, your determination. You're so much like your mother. I know she's watching you now amongst the great cloud of witnesses and feeling proud, too.'

Rachel swallowed hard. Her grandmother's words meant the world to her at that moment.

'Tradition says you don't wear white if you're not a virgin,' a lady in the bridal shop had told Rachel as she searched for a wedding dress. But Prince had shaken his head when he heard the idea.

'Remember what we've been learning at church, Rach? In Christ you are a spotless bride. You are holy and blameless. And besides, white suits you.' His last words were said with a smile, and Rachel knew that now nothing would stop her wearing white.

So she stood wearing the white wedding dress with poise and confidence. Maybe she didn't deserve to wear it, but because of all Jesus had done for her, she was worthy.

A commotion began outside the door and Rachel looked up. Someone rushed in and she found herself caught up in a fierce hug.

'Kylie! You're here?'

Kylie stepped back and though her smile stretched across her face, tears flowed down her cheeks. 'You didn't think I'd miss this day, did you? We're sisters, remember?'

'But it's such a long way to come. I didn't want to ask that of you.'

'I know. But Grandma did.' She threw Grandma Blythe a look of appreciation. 'Thanks, Grandma.' She stepped back from Rachel and swiped at her eyes and the mascara now running down her face. 'I admit that at first I was hurt, thinking you were still shutting me out like when your parents died, but then I realised that in some crazy way you think you're looking after us all, don't you? You try to protect us from what you're going through, but we want to be a part of it, Rach. We want to be part of your life. You didn't let me be there for you when your Mum and Dad died, but I won't let you shut me out anymore. I'm going to go through this day with you and I'm going to be here for you when you have your babies!'

Rachel opened and shut her mouth a few times, then smiled as warmth filled her heart. Somewhere along the way Kylie had grown up. Or maybe it was her.

'Promise me?' Kylie whispered.

'I promise.'

Kylie stood straight and smoothed back her hair which had been ruffled by her fierce hug. 'And I hope you don't mind, but I've brought my boyfriend. I figure Prince won't be jealous, so it won't matter.' She giggled. 'He's Irish and has a really strong accent, so when he talks, just pretend you understand him, okay?'

Rachel chuckled and nodded. It was so good to see Kylie again. Grandma Blythe gave them both a fierce hug, then took Rachel's hand.

'Okay, time to go. No more tears. Grandpa will be waiting for us.'

As Rachel walked down the aisle beside her grandfather, she looked nervously at the dozen faces watching her. And then her eyes met with those of Bonnie Blake, the popular girl she had been to school with so many years ago. Burns or no burns, Bonnie Blake was beautiful. Those wide blue eyes shone with a peace and joy Rachel had never believed humanly possible.

She truly does know God! Rachel thought, and peace stole over her. Another answered prayer. All the anguish, the shadowy clouds which had seemed to engulf her as she struggled in prayer. Yes, it had all been worth it.

Then she looked to the front to where stood the most handsome man she had ever seen. She caught her breath in a gasp and would have run to his arms had her grandfather not held her back.

'Steady,' he whispered. 'He's not going anywhere.'

Rachel giggled, then saw Prince match her smile with his. Then his smile slowly widened into a grin, the one she had learned to love. Yes, God's wonderful mercies were new every morning.

***

Guests gathered around an afternoon tea and Rachel turned to see Bonnie Blake at her side. The only burn marks now visible were on Bonnie's hands and arms and the joy radiating from her wide blue eyes was captivating.

'Rachel, you're beautiful.' Bonnie gave her a hug.

Rachel found it ironic that the girl whose appearance and confidence she had most envied all through school was now calling her beautiful. Emotion threatened to overwhelm her as she returned the hug.

'Thank you.' She stepped back and studied Bonnie. 'You know, I prayed for you every day since your accident. I could hardly believe it when I heard you had become a believer.'

Bonnie laughed. 'Why, because I was such a delinquent at school?'

'Ah, so you admit it!' a teasing voice said, and both turned to see Blaze standing there. 'Congratulations, sister.' He bent to give Rachel a quick kiss on the cheek and Rachel tried not to stare. Blaze had changed. All his pimples had gone and somehow between now and the last time she had seen him, he had become a man.

Blaze turned to his wife. 'And congratulations on gaining a new sister-in-law.' He gave Bonnie a teasing smile then gave her a passionate kiss on the lips. Rachel laughed, feeling awkward at the display of affection, but also hoping that someday she and Prince would share the same kind of relationship. A female voice interrupted her thoughts.

'So I hear you're going to provide us with a niece and nephew.'

The girl before her had a familiar face yet Rachel couldn't place her except to recognise she was one of the Clements and was by far the most beautiful girl she had ever seen. Immediately her face clouded. How could Prince be attracted to her with such relatives?

The girls seemed to sense Rachel's discomfort. 'Remember me? I'm Beauty.'

'Beauty,' Rachel repeated, stunned. 'Wow, you've changed.'

Beauty smiled, and then Rachel realised what it was. Beauty's sullen, defensive attitude was now nonexistent. Her face sported an open, accepting expression that drew Rachel to her.

'I know God now,' Beauty explained. 'I'm nothing like that spiteful girl I was at school. Thank God!'

Rachel smiled at Beauty's description of herself, then tried to mask her surprise as Beauty put a hand on her arm. 'Rachel, don't let guilt get to you.' Those dark eyes so like Prince's were imploring her to understand. 'That was my whole problem – guilt that I was alive when my mother wasn't. Guilt that I was so unlovable, that I killed a little boy ... all kinds of things. Don't listen to it!'

Rachel finally found her tongue. 'Thanks,' she whispered, overcome.

But Beauty wasn't finished. 'God has forgiven. That's all

that matters. Even when Christians mess up, God forgives. Just ask Blaze. He can tell you all about it.'

Rachel wondered if Beauty meant Blaze had messed up or just that Blaze knew it could happen. She wasn't given a chance to ask.

'I'm so glad God brought you into our family.' Beauty's face transformed into a smile, and Rachel couldn't look away. 'I prayed for someone like you to bring Prince to know God. And God picked you because he knew no one could do it like you could.'

'Do what?' Prince had come to Rachel's side.

'Kiss,' Beauty responded cheekily, causing Rachel's cheeks to become a fiery red.

'Is that right?' Prince seemed amused by her embarrassment. 'Let me see.'

Rachel tried to pull away, aware that Beauty was watching, but the beautiful girl just laughed in delight as Prince held his new wife tight and kissed her deeply.

'I think you're right,' Prince spoke to his sister but didn't take his eyes from Rachel's. 'Nobody kisses like she does.'

'And you ought to know,' Beauty retorted. 'You've kissed so many girls.'

With reflexes like lightning, Prince spun around and lifted his sister high on his shoulder, paying little concern to the formal clothes she was wearing.

'You be careful, little sister,' he warned. 'I haven't lost my circus talent and I can still run and ride faster than you ever could.'

'Put me down!' She struggled fiercely and beat on his shoulders but even Rachel could hear the laughter in her voice.

'Only if you promise to never mention the past again.'

She smiled fully, still struggling to get free of her brother's grasp. 'But Prince, the past is what makes us who we are now. Without the past we couldn't look back and see the incredible work of God which has made us who we are.'

Prince lowered his sister to the ground and his eyes met with

Rachel's before he faced his sister again. 'You're right, Beauty.'

'Of course I'm right.' Beauty primly straightened her dress, looking for all the world like a princess, and then suddenly flew at her brother, attempting to tackle him.

He shook his head and laughed as he lifted her again and carried her a few metres away to where Blaze stood with Bonnie. He dumped her at Blaze's feet.

'Deal with her, would you, big brother? She's become unruly and disorderly since she's been living with you.'

With that, he turned back to join Rachel, whose eyes were shining. God truly had blessed her with a wonderful family and a husband she admired and respected more and more each day.

CHAPTER THIRTY TWO

Rachel sat before the uni church congregation, her eyes resting on each person, one by one. They sat perfectly still, waiting for what she had to say.

'I have a song I want to sing for you.' She gently touched the piano keys, but didn't press them. 'But first I want to share with you what brought me to write such a song of praise and thanks to God.'

She took a deep breath, glancing to where Prince sat listening intently. He smiled slowly and Rachel smiled back, warmth filling her as it did every time those dark eyes met with hers. His look gave her courage.

'Prince and I have just returned from our honeymoon. But we are seven months pregnant with twins.' She adjusted the microphone before her, then forced herself to look out at the congregation again. 'If, as a teenager, I had been told I would fall into temptation and have sex before marriage, I would not have believed it. Somehow I thought I was exempt from that kind of temptation because I was a Christian and my father was a minister.'

She knew her voice was shaking but was determined to go on.

'Prince was not a Christian when it all happened and it wasn't like it had been building up for a while or that I wasn't walking with God. I had spent time with him that very morning. Prince and I weren't even romantically involved. I had just had a bad day and my human side took over. I did something I never believed I would do.'

'So don't ever believe you are stronger than any temptation.' She wiped sweaty hands down her skirt. 'Be on your guard, always aware that it is only in God's strength we stand!'

Then her voice became quieter. 'But if you fall, always remember God's forgiveness is available if you ask for it. But not only his forgiveness. His mercy. I am so aware that it is only by God's mercy that I am where I am today. The father of my children could have been a drug addict, a violent man who would never care for me, or someone who would never come to know the Lord. Then where would I be?'

'And yet, I know there are no "what ifs" in God's plan. He knew I would fall and he was waiting there to catch me. God's mercies are greater than my mistakes! That is the reason for my song.'

With that, she took a deep breath, touched the piano keys and began to play. Her heart swelled as the moving melody overcame her nerves. She began to sing:

'God's wonderful mercies are new every morning,
complete and secure in every day's dawning.
Never left sinking in the down of the sun,
never left hidden behind all you've done.
Forgiveness for hatred and love for your pain,
purpose for failure and sun through the rain.
Lifting the clouds he will answer your prayer,
Promising always his mercy is there.'

***

Rachel stepped away from the piano, wondering at the complete silence. Then applause broke out. She turned to smile at the congregation and saw several people wiping away tears. Her heart welled with gratefulness and love for Jesus, her closest friend who had given so much for her. And she knew that truly, she had been forgiven much so she could love much.

***

Prince and Rachel discussed the evening in the quiet of their home. Prince laid a gentle hand on her stomach and Rachel felt the kicks he received. He moved his hand again and laughed as he received an even stronger kick. 'We should name them something like Mercy.'

Rachel giggled. 'One's a boy, remember?'

He gave her a poke. 'You *know* I'm talking about our daughter.' Then he became serious. 'But we haven't even discussed names.'

Rachel nodded. 'I've thought of a few.'

'You have? You never said anything.'

'No, because they're *our* children. You should get to name at least one.'

'Maybe, but there's no harm in making suggestions. What names did you come up with?'

Feeling self-conscious, she wondered what he would think of the names she thought of. But he had asked. She lifted her chin in determination. 'Seton for the boy and Blythe for the girl.' Quickly she went on to explain. 'I don't want my parents to be forgotten. So I used their surnames. Blythe was Mum's maiden name.'

Prince nodded, while she hurried on. 'But I'll just name our daughter if you choose the name for the boy.'

'Okay,' he gave his slow smile. 'I choose Seton.'

'But Prince –'

'You said I could choose. That's my choice.'

'But didn't you have some ideas of your own?'

'No,' he chuckled. 'My family are better at choosing names for horses and it's a tradition I don't really want to carry on.'

'So you didn't have anything planned?'

A mischievous look came to his eyes. 'I had thought of "Pure Aggression" or "Broken Nose" or "Lion Eyes" but I thought you might object.'

Rachel burst into giggles and Prince ended up laughing with

her. She snuggled into his arms. 'You know, ever since the day I met you, I dreamed of someday marrying you.'

'Really?' Prince held her closer against his chest. 'So now your dreams have come true?'

'Not really. It's nothing like I dreamed.'

'What was your dream, then?' Prince pulled back so he could see her face.

'Well, first, you'd see some of my poems and be really impressed,' she gave a rueful smile. 'Then I'd accidentally drop one that I wrote about you and you'd find it. You'd become a Christian. Then you'd realise you were in love with me. We'd have a wonderful romance, become engaged, get married and *then* have children.'

Prince nodded seriously and she was glad he didn't laugh at her dream.

'It all happened back to front, didn't it?' he said. 'First we conceived a child, then I fell in love with you, and then I became a Christian. And the more I get to know you, the more I admire and respect you. I can't imagine life without you.'

Rachel sat up. 'You fell in love with me before you gave your life to God?' She stared at him, clinging to the words of hope that were a lifeline.

'Did I say that?' Prince looked sheepish.

'You did.'

'Well, I guess I'd better confess, then.' His mouth tilted in the corners. 'Yes, I fell in love with you. And that day you came to tell me you were pregnant I couldn't kid myself anymore. When I asked if you had to marry me, I wanted you to say yes so badly. I didn't realise how badly until you said no. I guess I probably loved you before then but that's when I realised it.'

Her glowing eyes sparkled with tears as she drew in a deep breath. Prince took her hand. 'Did I say something wrong?'

'No.' She sniffled. 'It's just I was so scared that you might not really love me. Not the way I long to be loved. I thought our marriage was just …'

'A marriage of obligation? Of convenience?'

'Yes.'

'No, my Rachel.' He kissed away her tears. 'I love you more than I know how to tell you.'

Rachel smiled widely as she gazed into his dark eyes, then a frown passed over her face.

Prince reached a finger to try to smooth the wrinkles in her forehead. 'What's that look about?'

She shrugged. 'I don't know. I'm just wondering, did God show himself to you because of my prayers for you or did God tell me to pray for you *because* you were always going to be his child?'

He smiled. 'I would say a bit of both. I guess we'll never know until we get to heaven but it's like the question about whether God made me be born into a family with believers because I would become one or whether I became one *because* of my family. It's a whole other issue I don't want to get into right now. Let's just believe our Father God is in control and leave it at that.'

Rachel nodded. 'You're right. We'll never know until we get to heaven, though I'm certain that question will be far from the first thing on our minds when we get there.'

As she spoke, her face lit with joy, for this time her anticipation for reaching her final home was not because she wanted so badly to see her beloved parents again. It was because she knew on that day she would see Jesus face to face. She would be warmly welcomed by her beloved friend who loved her so deeply he died for her, though he knew how much she hurt him. She would approach his throne as a spotless bride wearing pure white.

ALSO BY JENNY GLAZEBROOK

Aussie Sky Series
Blaze in the Storm
Heart of Thunder

COMING SOON

Mist of the Morning
Book 4 Aussie Sky Series
Release 2015

Roy can't work out if clumsy Misty Clements is clever and manipulative or if she is just as lost in the world as she seems. What is she hiding from him?

www.ingramcontent.com/pod-product-compliance
Lightning Source LLC
Chambersburg PA
CBHW031241120726
47905CB00002B/683